the PRINCIPLES of L♥VE

All You Need Is Love

Emily Franklin

nal
jam
books

NAL Jam
Published by New American Library, a division of Penguin Group (USA) Inc.,
375 Hudson Street, New York, New York 10014, USA
Penguin Group (Canada), 90 Eglinton Avenue East, Suite 700, Toronto,
Ontario M4P 2Y3, Canada (a division of Pearson Penguin Canada Inc.)
Penguin Books Ltd., 80 Strand, London WC2R 0RL, England
Penguin Ireland, 25 St. Stephen's Green, Dublin 2, Ireland (a division of Penguin Books Ltd.)
Penguin Group (Australia), 250 Camberwell Road, Camberwell, Victoria 3124,
Australia (a division of Pearson Australia Group Pty. Ltd.)
Penguin Books India Pvt. Ltd., 11 Community Centre, Panchsheel Park,
New Delhi - 110 017, India
Penguin Group (NZ), cnr Airborne and Rosedale Roads, Albany,
Auckland 1310, New Zealand (a division of Pearson New Zealand Ltd.)
Penguin Books (South Africa) (Pty.) Ltd., 24 Sturdee Avenue,
Rosebank, Johannesburg 2196, South Africa

Penguin Books Ltd., Registered Offices:
80 Strand, London WC2R 0RL, England

First published by NAL Jam, an imprint of New American Library,
a division of Penguin Group (USA) Inc.

First Printing, September 2006
10　9　8　7　6　5　4　3　2　1

NAL JAM and logo are trademarks of Penguin Group (USA) Inc.

LIBRARY OF CONGRESS CATALOGING-IN-PUBLICATION DATA:

Franklin, Emily.
　[Principles of love]
　All you need is love: the principles of love/Emily Franklin.
　　p. cm.
　ISBN 0-451-21961-9 (trade pbk.)
　[1. Coming of age—Fiction. 2. Fathers and daughters—Fiction. 3. Aunts—Fiction. 4.
Boarding schools—Fiction. 5. Schools—Fiction. 6. Massachusetts—Fiction.] I. Title.

PZ7.F8583A11 2006
[Fic]—dc22　　　　2006002274

Set in Bembo • Designed by Elke Sigal

Printed in the United States of America

For my grandparents,
who continue to teach me so much about love

Acknowledgments

Thank you to Adam and the kids and to my extended family, for enthusiasm and support. Smiles, nods, and thanks to my editor, Anne Bohner. To Faye Bender, exemplary agent and Labello-lover, thanks and more.

Chapter 1

I currently have the feeling that I'm living in some twisted dream: I keep waiting to wake up and find out everything that's happened in the past days—okay, nearly a week—was just some side effect of bad sushi.

Except that I don't really like sushi (okay, I like the California rolls, but that's all). And so the chances of suffering a long-term, raw-fish-induced nightmare session are slim. The reality of my life right now is this: I'm curled up in bed under my plain white sheets, pretending to sleep so my dad doesn't make me get up and play a six a.m. game of squash with him. To fight his stress level and possibly to keep his physique in top form for his new girlfriend, he's been all about cardio activity. He knows my body clock (among other things) is off and once he hears me wandering around up here, he knocks on my door with his squash racket and tries to convince me to get court-bound.

"Endorphins help the body relax," he explained during our game last night. The courts were locked but he opened the heavy blue metal door with his master key and held it for me. "Squash is my yoga."

"Sounds like a bumper sticker," I said and proceeded to get my butt whipped (figuratively speaking, of course) by my dad. There were shots I could have hit, and plenty I could have at least made the effort to reach, but I was—am—so distracted I could hardly remember to tie my shoes, let alone get my hand-eye coordination to comply.

So now I'm in bed, trying to lull myself back into a REM cycle, but failing. Sleep is my yoga. Except not. I've been here (here=Hadley Hall in all its prep school springtime glory, not my bed) for around a week, having left London and my finally gush-worthy love life behind, but I haven't succeeded in registering the departure in my brain. Somehow I can't accept that I'm not going back.

Pining for the luxurious yet understated flat I shared with Arabella, my classes that stimulated my mind and thoughts of my future, and the independent life I left across the Atlantic has been draining. Plus, visiting Aunt Mable at the hospital has made the days here have the antithetical feeling of Vacation Flyby Syndrome (VFS=that feeling that anything fun just flew by so fast you hardly had time to appreciate it), leaving me with Sudden Reality Syndrome (SRS), where you're sucked back into the normalcy of your everyday life. So I've had a big-time case of VFS, even though London wasn't a vacation exactly, and I've been way bogged down by an even bigger case of SRS that's left me semihumorless and hermitlike.

I've been nearly one hundred percent successful in avoiding social run-ins on campus. I feel ghostly visiting there—like I'm semiseen—but since I haven't been a fixture at Hadley for a whole semester, it's as though I don't count. Plus, I'm still way jet-lagged. Who knew a five-hour time change could mess with my brain state quite so much? I vaguely remember the feeling of landing in London and being overwhelmed with the need for sleep, but coming back is worse.

I'm so tired at night I've gone to bed no later than eight o'clock, and my mornings begin promptly at four, which is nine a.m. in England. I'm living the life of an infant, except no one's singing me to sleep or rocking me as the sun rises. Mainly, this is because I'm not a newborn, but it's also because the person who would have me in his arms isn't here. He's three thousand miles away.

I check my watch. By now, Asher Piece, the English love of my life, is probably on his fifth cup of tea at his gallery. I can see him in his oh-so-adorable clothing, traditional button-downs that are always slightly rumpled, hair that's determined to mis-behave, and that smile. That mouth. Those lips. Those lips I won't be kissing for a long time. But before I get carried away with too many scenarios involving Asher appearing at my door and waking me with kisses, my sleep-deprived self arrives back at the true reality of my sudden return to prep school. Plus, I'm already awake, so that pretty much nixes that romantic scenario.

I stare at the ceiling and look for patterns in the plaster the way Dad and I used to look for shapes in the clouds. Mable. Aunt Mable is not doing well. I would say she's doing badly but then I feel like I'm jinxing the situation, so I just tell my-self that things are tough right now. Cue mental image of Mable lying in her hospital room, slipping in and out of consciousness, her face bony, her skin sallow and bruised from all the tubes and needles. Tears rush down my cheeks, dampening my pillows and making my nose run. I sit up, look for a tissue, but find none, so I use the snot-factor as reason to rise and not-so-much shine as brood.

Out the window, the fields are bright green and empty. The assembly bell won't ring for another hour, and most students are sleeping. Later, the Hadley Hallers will traipse to class slowly, reveling in their springtime-induced leisure. Yesterday, in a quick walk around campus (I've been avoiding putting in too much face time), it was easy to spot the usual signs that spring has sprung, that we're in the last push of the school year: hand-holding is de rigueur for couples and uncouples, backpacks strewn on the quad, seniors tempting the disciplinary gods by sitting on the science building roof, sophomore girls showing way too much skin as they sun themselves near the LOG. The Lowenthal Outdoor Gymnasium opens its giant garage-style door (it rolls up on nice days) so people can pump up and down on the treadmill half in, half out of doors.

I, meanwhile, am holed up in my room like it's still winter. Which maybe, in my mind, it still is. Or rather, I'm still a season back, in London with Arabella and Asher and Fizzy and Keena and my wonderful mentor, Poppy Massa-Tonclair, one of the greatest living writers. Of course, the mention of her name (did I mention it? Am I talking out loud? Note to self: Seek help) brings to mind all of the work I left behind in London.

But as I look at the photograph on my bureau, the one of me and Mable dressed like trashy extras from a big-hair video circa 1986, I put aside thoughts of my recent past and focus on what's in front of me. The picture is just a tiny reminder of such a funny day: Mable convinced me to don a lycra tube dress, so tight she had to roll it on me, and she wore an electric blue spandex all in one, and we walked up and down Newbury Street—aka fashion central—and laughed our asses off for no good reason other than it was damn humorous. I put the photo next to my bed and sigh.

I'm glad I'm here. I need to be back here and be with Mable—for better or for worse—she needs me and I need to feel that I'm in proximity to her, even if she's not aware that I'm with her.

Just as I've mustered up the energy to go get some cardio-yoga-love myself, the phone rings. I reach for it and sit at my computer, figuring I can multitask and print my assignments from London while talking.

"Is this the residence of a Miss Bee-you-cow-sky?" Asher enunciates each syllable so it sounds like he's in slow motion.

"Let me see if she's here," I say in an overly American nasal voice—and manage to convince him I'm someone else.

"Oh, terribly sorry—I thought . . . ," he stammers.

"It's me, fool," I say. "Just a few days apart and you can't even recognize my voice?"

"Believe me, you don't sound like that normally." Asher sighs. I can hear street noise in the background.

"And how do I sound normally?" I ask and miss him so much it's all I can do to keep myself from ditching everything and hailing a cab to the airport and back to London and into his arms.

"Lovely. That's how you sound," Asher says.

"Where are you?" I ask. "Describe your location so I can picture it."

"Well, let me see. I'm looking around and it appears as though I'm on the corner of . . . no—can't quite make out that street sign. Anyway, I'm in Hackney in front of a statue of a rather rude horse and rider. I'm meeting a client for lunch." Then there's a pause. I wonder if it's one of those romantic pauses where we're both thinking back on our time together or remembering kissing in front of a different statue or—if maybe the pause is one of those awkward ones.

"I miss you," I say and then feel like I've put too much on the table.

"I miss you so much, Love. Really, it's crap here without you," Asher says and makes me feel completely at ease, which of course makes me miss him more, but I don't say that.

Instead, I print all my essay and work assignments that Arabella emailed me and say, "So—who's the lucky fellow?"

"Huh?" Asher's phone beeps, signaling another call coming in. The fact that the whole world doesn't know we're on the phone and having an important call is unbelievable to me—who would dare to interrupt? "I'm not going to get that. What were you saying?"

"I said who's the lucky guy who gets your attention over lunch at some swanky but not so put together as to appear overdone café?"

"Very good marks on your description," Asher says and I

can hear the low blurble of noise intensify. "I'm in that café as
we speak."

"What's it called?" I want to know everything he's doing,
what he's eating, his exact locale, as though having that knowledge will help ease the distance.

"Café Alba. Should be a lovely meal. Cutting edge meets
country home food—not too avant-garde and not to lowbrow.
Oh—I've got to run—my client's here!"

"What's his name?" I ask. I like knowing all the names of
Asher's up-and-coming artists; they're the ones I suspect (like
he is) will rule the art world in a decade. Probably Asher's photos will be as famous as the Ansel Adams ones that grace the
walls of many a Hadley dorm.

"She," Asher corrects. "Valentine Green. She's a total nutter, but very talented."

I can hear said nutter kiss the cheek of my boyfriend and I
grow, yes, green with envy. Of course, I don't give in to my
sudden need to know if Valentine is long-limbed and gorgeous; I just wish him a good lunch. "Talk to you soon?"

Asher blows a kiss into the phone. The fact that he'd do this
in public in front of a client makes me blush. "I'll give you a
ring ASAP," he says. "And we'll plan my trip over."

I taught him the expression "as soon as possible," and its ab-
breviation, ASAP. It's now said with slightly too much fre-
quency, but right now, it doesn't bug me because Asher is
coming to visit! I do a little dance and imagine introducing
him to Mable and how she'd clutch my hand and say out loud
how incredibly hot he is, just to embarrass me.

"Okay—remember the time change when you call—just so you don't wake my dad."

When you're so used to being around someone the way I got used to being with Asher, it's impossible not to think of what they're doing all the time. If I'm snacking on graham crackers, he's having dinner; if I'm waking up, he's at work.

"I'll talk to you soon," I say, but realize I can't compute *soon* into hours or minutes or days.

We hang up and I make a pact to get myself together. At least partially.

As I gather up my printed matter and try not to panic at the amount of work I need to finish (finish=start), I make a POA. My Plan of Action for this week is as follows: LOG for some much-needed flabercise (read: no running, wine drinking, and lovely English puddings have made my jeans just a bit too tight), hours and hours of solid work at the library, visits to Mable at Mass General, and my much-dreaded meeting with Academic Affairs (why does the office have such a romantic name when it's just a holding pen for failure??) to determine the fallout from leaving London early. Then I'll probably see my dad for dinner and crawl into bed by eight again.

Maybe tonight I'll make it until nine. Which is two in the morning in London. When will I stop computing the time change and wondering what's happening there, what I'm missing? Maybe when the doors of reality open and welcome me inside.

Chapter 2

The doors of reality in this case are the large double arches (no, not of artery-clogging fast food) of Master's Hall. Set back from the main campus, Master's looks small compared to the grand pillared style of the ivy-covered brick buildings used for classes. Once the headmaster's office (once=1790-something), it is now the site of formal investigations into academic doings or undoings. Not to be confused with the Discipline Committee that meets elsewhere (and with my father, I might add), the Academic Committee (or the AC as they're known) meets in one small room that, despite its ventilated name, is known for its intense humidity.

As soon as I walk through the doors, I'm sweating. Droplets of perspiration make their way from my workout bra to my belly button and I hope I don't look nervous—just overheated.

"Please, take a seat," says Mrs. Hendricks, the remarkably nonsweaty ACC. "I've elected to handle your case myself as George Humphries is dealing with another matter." Not sure what that "other matter" is—I'm too out of the Hadley Gossip Loop these days—but I'm thrilled to have Mrs. Hendricks. She has a reputation for being kind and gentle with her cases.

"The fact that I have a case seems really unsettling," I say. Last semester, a senior in my ethics class realized she was three semesters shy of completing her math requirement, and once she explained her situation to Hendricks, all she had to do was some Saturday tutorials. I'm hoping for something easy, too, given the circumstances.

As if she reads my mind Mrs. Hendricks says, "Given the circumstances, I believe you did the best thing." She gives me a small smile from across the desk and I notice her pink ribbon pinned to her sweater. Everyone knows someone or is connected to someone with breast cancer and it's comforting not to feel so alone.

"I'm so glad you see my point of view," I say. "My aunt is— she's very important to me as I'm sure my dad explained. So there's really no way I could stay abroad and miss . . ." My voice starts to crack. I will myself not to cry.

"Love—I understand the circumstances and as I said, I agree with you. Were I in your position I would likely do the same thing."

I sigh, glad I won't be penalized. "Great. So do I just make my college counseling appointments and audit classes?"

Mrs. Hendricks shakes her head. "I'm afraid it's not that simple, Love. LADAM won't give you credit because you're not actually attending their program."

I lick my lips and feel the sweat gather in my bra. "But they gave me assignments. My friend Arabella Piece—the exchange student who was here—emailed me all the work I've missed and I can do it all here and send papers back . . ."

"But LADAM won't accept all of them!" Mrs. Hendricks allows her voice to get stern. "You don't seem to grasp the full situation, Love."

"No, I guess I don't. I left London really suddenly and no one told me about the problems that would cause." My hair slips from its loose knot and the red of it covers my eyes. I quickly tuck it behind my ears and try to think fast. "Can't I do the Hadley work?"

"You're not a registered student at Hadley this term," Mrs. Hendricks explains. She looks for something in one of the antiquated files that form a U-shape into which her desk is tucked.

"So basically, I'm a woman without a country, with no school, and yet lots of requirements to fulfill," I say. "And since Hadley has no summer school, I wouldn't graduate for a year and a half? Nothing I did in London would count?"

"Yes, I should think that sums it up rather well. In the fine print of your application to LADAM, it states that work must be completed in full and in person in order for any of the credit to count." In her cotton cardigan and sensible skirt, Mrs. Hendricks comes around to my side of the table. "Now, ordinarily, I would be the first to tell you that you've made your academic bed and now you must lie in it. But due to the nature of your decision to come back, I think we need to find a solution."

I manage a smile. Maybe I won't have to be the oldest senior ever at Hadley. "Suggestions?"

"I've taken the liberty of speaking with"—she looks at the paper in her hands—"Poppy Massa-Tonclair. Quite a name. Anyway, she gave you such a glowing review that I asked her to sponsor you in an ISPP." She pronounces this last term iss-pee, like a snake with a bladder problem in the punch line of a joke, but I refrain from commenting on it.

"I've never actually known anyone who did an ISPP," I say. "They're sort of mythical on campus." Rumor had it that one guy Something Something Addison (one of those cool board-ing students of legendary status) who graduated years before got one for doing a nonprofit project, but until now I assumed it was campus lore.

"They're extremely rare. For extenuating circumstances only and I believe this qualifies." Mrs. Hendricks hands the paper to me and I look at the paragraphs that describe my project.

"PMT—I mean—Poppy Massa-Tonclair said she'd do this? Really?"

Mrs. Hendricks nods. "The final project is due in duplicate to this office. You'll need to send another copy to LADAM. Any of the work you've been assigned through your London courses is up to you to consider—it's not a technical require-ment, but it would serve your record well to complete it any-way. Good luck."

Serve my record well? So the reality is that I have more work than before. Well, it's better than repeating half of junior year. I stand up, convinced I've lost those extra London pounds by sheer loss of water-weight. "Thanks—thanks so much!"

•   •   •

"So you're basically making a movie for credit while I have to slog through academic hell, otherwise known as calculus and advanced Latin?" Chris asks as we do nonimpact heavy cardio on the elliptical trainers at the LOG.

"Hey—my movie, as you call it, is just an idea right now. And no one forced you to take advanced Latin—you just signed up because that guy you thought was hot was in it."

Chris swats my shoulder. "I told you that in confidence!" His look these days is a perfect melding of the 1950's prepster (think: black-and-white photos of guys in Madras on the porch of some summer estate) and leftist cool (think Elvis Costello glasses and roughed-up seams on all his pants).

"Like there's anyone around," I say and gesture to the empty gym. "Which is a shame only because if there's no one here, there's no one to appreciate how great you're looking these days."

Chris quickens his pace and smiles. "It's so good to have you back—I missed my fan club." He breathes hard. "You know you're the only member of that club, right?"

"I hardly think that," I say and check how many minutes I've been ellipticalling. Not enough for that endorphin release.

We have the most coveted spots in the LOG, the row of machines that face directly onto the quad, perfect for people-peering and taking my mind off my woes.

"Blah—I'm so relieved—Mrs. Hendricks seriously made me think I wouldn't graduate next year." I get off the machine and go to the weight training center, which is far enough away

from where Chris is that I have to yell a little. Or whatever the
word is before yelling.

"It's not like the film will be easy—I mean, first of all, PMT
has to approve my whole idea. And she might not, given the
fact that she is, in fact, a professor of LITERATURE." I work
my thighs and then pause between sets. "Then I have to think
of a topic, an angle, a whole way of making it coherent. Which
is why a movie makes the most sense."

"And what will this Oscar-winning viewing experience be
about?" Chris yells back.

"I don't know yet," I say. More sweat drips from my forehead, my hair is greasy and matted, and my face has that
blotchy, hot itchy feeling—a sort of allergy season meets de-
odorant ad. I am SO sexy. "What's a good plot for a movie?"

Then, from behind me:

"Why don't you make a movie about how much better
things were around here when you were gone?"

The words alone could belong to anyone with dire need of
butt-pole removal, but the sultry, nasty voice comes attached to
none other than the bitch-on-wheels Lindsay Parrish. Evil in-
carnate is close enough to smell—and I have to admit her
scent is kind of appealing—like one part Upper East Side expensive perfume, the other like freesia; how anyone so mean
got to smell so good is beyond me. Then again, the world's not
a fair place, is it? The smell of her is enough to send my mind
reeling (ha-ha, film reference) back to her cruelty last term, the
way she and Cordelia (aka faculty brat extraordinaire) tried to
condemn me in front of the whole school at my play. The way

Lindsay made Arabella—my best friend—run naked around the flagpole. The way she tried to steal my old boyfriend, Jacob. And the minute I think this, I all of a sudden realize, she might have succeeded.

Chris comes over to stop the slur-slinging before it starts. "Hey, Lindsay," he says and eyes her fancy workout attire. "Did you not get the memo that you can't bring bitches into the gym?"

"If you mean dogs, then your fake girlfriend here should leave."

"Enough," I say and hold up my hand and turn to Chris. "She's so not worth it."

"Funny." Lindsay cocks her head and smiles wickedly, her teeth bleached and ready for the kill. "That's just what Jacob said about you when he and I first hooked up."

I don't give her the credit of responding, but when I drop Chris at his class and head home to shower, I have that rush of TISHS (Things I Should Have Said). I should have told Lindsay that it doesn't matter to me what happened with her and Jacob. That I knew they hooked up while I was in London—yes, London, Lindsay, with my hot aristocratic boyfriend. Did I mention he's amazing, and out of every girl in the entire small though highly populated British Isles, he chose me?

I wash off the remains of the morning's sweat and sludge in the shower and picture Asher coming for his promised visit. Am I totally shallow for wanting to parade him up and down the quad, to make out with him in front of Lindsay so she can drool and then go home and pick her zits (okay, maybe she has one—somewhere) and doubt her self-worth? Perhaps this wish is surface level, but I hate the fact that I'm back here dealing with anvil-heavy issues and Lindsay can come along and knock me down with one phrase.

As I towel my hair dry and consider various subjects for my ISPP, I realize I have yet to set up my college counseling meeting with Mrs. Dandy-Patinko, so I decide to go over there on my way to Mass General. So much for putting in solid study hours at the library. As a compromise, I shove some books in my bag and head out the door, trying not to admit the real reason Lindsay's words bugged me.

The real reason being, of course, that I have unresolved issues with Jacob. Not with Lindsay. Lindsay's a known entity—nothing she does or says or inflicts should be surprising. But Jacob—he's the one I thought I knew. And yet I never would have predicted he'd fall prey to Lindsay's hot body and mean spirit. For some reason I put his morals and desires above the random hookup.

The college counseling building remains, comfortingly— annoying—the exact same as when I left. Sturdy bookcases filled with college catalogs, pamphlets, leaflets, lots of lets, and yet none that reads, "This Is Where Love Should Apply, Be Accepted, and Go."

Only as I wait for Mrs. Dandy-Patinko to free herself from the tangle of her headphones do I admit it—not even in my journal because putting it on paper would make it too real. In my mind I say, very small, like I'm talking to myself in lower-case—*Lindsay hooked up with Jacob.* He hasn't been pining for me. He has put his mouth, which is lovely full but not too full so as to be pouchy—on her mouth. She probably had her hands tucked into his dark mop of curls.

Never mind that I've been kissing—and beyond—close to sleeping with Asher. And never mind that I haven't even seen Jacob in almost a year. But the thought of him with Lindsay makes my stomach turn. The other students waiting for college counseling don't look at me as I seethe; they're all too focused on their own problems—SATs, college interviews (um, hello, note to self: Need to get butt in gear for those and feet in non-flip-flops to make studious impression), and the dreaded SIBOF scores that Hadley uses to Magic Eight Ball your college track. Maybe they predict where you'll get in so they can claim "very high acceptance rates to students' top choice colleges" in their catalog. Hey, maybe my brain is finally off the thaw status and back to thinking clearly (until seven thirty tonight when I crash and lose the ability to do simple math).

Mrs. Dandy-Patinko, my good-natured bosomy college counselor, appears at the doorway to (no, not hell—that's Lindsay's dorm room in Fruckner House) her office. She straightens her hair and smiles—one of us is the lucky person who is next in line to focus on their futures.

"I'm ready for Love!" Mrs. Dandy-Patinko announces.

Aren't we all?

"Hello," the now–face familiar head nurse on Mable's floor greets me in her hushed tones at the nurses' station. "Before your visit today, we'd like to have a word."

My heart races, my chest throbs, my knees threaten to buckle. I didn't tell my dad I was coming today, so there's no chance he would have prepared me for the worst—if that's what this is.

"Can I please just see my aunt?" I ask. I live in constant fear that one day I will come for a visit and she will just be gone. That panic response makes me edgy. "I really need to get in there." I make a move toward the corridor that leads to her room, but I'm stopped in my tracks by Nurse Insensitive who asks me to please take a seat in the waiting room.

I do as I'm told, surrounded by other anxious people connected by grief or worry. Someone hands me a cup of coffee without speaking—I wonder if she is here visiting a friend, her mother, or partner. Who knows? I nod a thank you and sip the tepid cup of Joe (note to self: Add *cup of Joe* to annoying phrase list in journal). No one's coffee is as good as Mable's. Slave to the Grind is the best. Of course I'm biased, but it's smooth, strong, and rich without being overbearing. Oh my God, I think; I sound like I'm describing Asher. After a couple more sips, I am greeted by a familiar and welcoming face, Margaret Randall, Mable's favorite nurse. She's also Henry Randall's (aka Preppy Vineyard Boy) aunt and really nice. She's become chummy with my dad and was friendly to me before I left for London.

"Love—it's good to see you." She shakes my hand and I'm thankful for the reminder of her first name. She's so down-to-earth it's funny to think of her as being related to Henry's dad, Trip Randall III, who owns half of the Vineyard (including the café where Slave to the Grind II is opening this summer).

"Hi, Margaret." She looks at me and I know she has bad news. I calm myself down by picking at the Styrofoam cup on not-Joe and breathe through my nose like I do when I'm running long-distance.

"As you know, Mable's been having a pretty rough time after the second mastectomy," Margaret says. It's clear from her soft tone and gentle way of touching my hand that she's done this before. I'm kicking myself for not taking Chris up on his offer to come with me. I just felt guilty asking him to drive yet again with me when he could be working, wallowing, or crushing on campus.

I nod at Margaret. "You can just say what you need to say. I probably know it already anyway."

Margaret's expression changes. "Oh, you do? Well, then, I think I say for everyone here that we're sorry. And we wish it had worked out."

I start to bawl. Margaret puts her arms around me. "Were you and Miles close?"

I pull back and look at her. "What?"

"You and Miles—Mable's fiancé—were you close with him? I know you were going to be a bridesmaid and . . ."

My world is spinning and I am close to barfing in the family lounge area. "I'm so confused—what are you talking about? How does Miles factor into anything if Mable's in a coma—or worse?" Even saying the words makes me need to sit down. My dad should be here with me. Isn't it illegal to tell bad news to a minor? I need an emotional judge for this ruling.

Margaret covers her face. "I'm so sorry, Love. On behalf of

Mass General and myself, I apologize that you inferred that. Mable is actually much better—she turned a corner last night and is up and talking."

I'm doing breathing that's close to mutt pants (note to self: Do not make joke about mutt pants being a new trend—first boot cut, now mutt pants). "So then, what's the bad news? Why the grief-talk?"

Margaret clicks her tongue. "She broke it off with Miles."

"Again?" I shake my head. "I don't care. Just let me see her."

"Of course," Margaret waits for me to stand up and leads me past the nurses' station and over the cold linoleum tiles toward Mable. "I think she thought you'd be upset, that you were looking forward to being in the wedding."

"That's the farthest thing from my mind," I say and walk through Mable's door to find her sitting up, spooning Jell-O from a small plastic cup into her mouth. Her face is still pale, her lips dry. She's cogent and cheerful, better than she has been since I've been back, and talks fast to prove it.

"I forgot how good raspberry flavor is!" Mable says and gestures with the wobbly dessert like it's champagne. "Of course, you probably spell flavor with a *u*—that's so British. Like neighbour and colour. I went through a horrid phase in my early twenties of spelling everything Britishly. I know. Britishly is not a word. But I did—I spelled color c-o-l-o-u-r and everything. So lame!" She smiles at me; a real, full-on smile, and I grin back.

"You're insane! It's like, I'm unconscious—no I'm not, now I'm awake and speed-speaking!" I say and rush over and hug her, careful not to do it too hard lest I disturb any of the tubes. I haven't seen her awake like this in so long; even when I visited before, she didn't really know I was there, although she did mumble a lot.

"I'm not insane—well, not completely. I'm so glad to see you, British Lady." She pats my hair and I feel her familiar hand on my head and start to cry. I'm just a flood these days and I can't help it.

"Oh no, Love." Mable lets me sob a little, Margaret excuses herself, and I just wail. "I'm okay. I'm going to be okay."

I sit up and sniffle, unable to let go of Mable's hand. "I'll tell you about the situation between me and Miles in a second. First, let's talk a little about this summer—Slave to the Grind is waiting for you."

"And Arabella, right? She can still come?"

"Of course," Mable says. Then she pulls the nurse button and I panic again. "It's nothing health-related, Love." When Margaret reappears Mable says, "Didn't you have something for Love?"

Margaret pulls an envelope out of her pocket and hands it to me. "My nephew Henry came by to visit Mable. He hoped to see you but I told him you were in London for a while. Anyway, he left this." Margaret's pager blips and she hurries out of the room.

Mable raises her eyebrows at me as I look at what Henry left for me and I roll my blues at her. "It's not like that. Henry's just a really nice guy."

The card reads:

Tried to find you at Brown again—you must be really busy—I never seem to catch you on campus. Hope your college trip abroad was enlightening but not so much that you stay there forever (we'd miss you stateside). Hope your aunt feels well and that this note finds you happy and at home.—Henry

Friendly, slightly formal, not too this, not too that.

"Yeah." I nod at the note. "He's just really nice."

"Sure—a really nice, handsome rich guy who is so kind he visits your sickly aunt while you're off partying in London."

"One—I didn't party in London. Okay, a little I did. And two, don't make me feel guilty that I wasn't here the whole time." I look into her eyes and she smirks.

"I wasn't guilt-tripping you. All I meant was, Henry seems pretty decent."

I shake my head and gather my hair up into a ponytail, then let it fall. Mable twirls the end of some strands. "I'm all set in the guy department," I say.

"Do they have that at Bloomingdale's these days? I thought you had to custom order them online. Silly me." She motions for me to help her with her pillow so she can lie flat. "All I'm saying is I've been out there a long time and sometimes when you think you're all set with romance, it vanishes."

My cheeks blush for no good reason. "I'm sure that happens. But with Asher—it's good. Things are good. I'm going to bring him to meet you when he visits." I pause and then Mable overlaps with me as I say, "Lucky him."

Song for the drive back home=Aztec Camera. The words *your head is happy but your heart's insane* make me nod. I know I'm doing the right thing, what I have to do, by being here, but I can't shrug the feeling that I'm missing out on everything in London. Storrow Drive slings by me, the twinkling lights of Harvard in the distance. It's hard to think about college and planning for four years that are more than a full twelve months away; who can know what I'll feel then, or where I'll be happy and find a new home?

I sing and drive and go past Slave to the Grind for a coffee that will aid me in my quest for staying up later than I have been. Inside, the place is hopping. Mable's hired a bother-sister team to run the place while she's unable to, and they seem to have the system down pat.

"Hey—you're the singer, right?" the brother asks me. I nod. "Doug Martin. I know, two first names." He smiles at me and gets his sister's attention.

"Ula," she says and shakes my hand. Unlike her brother she doesn't offer an explanation of her rather interesting name.

"As in oh-la-la?" I ask and smile.

"Yeah, like I haven't heard that before." Ula rolls her eyes. "No, as in Swedish heritage."

"Never mind my sister," Doug says. "She burned herself on the frother—you know what that's like."

"I do, actually. It sucks." I take out some money, more as a gesture than anything else. "Can I have a medium mocha, please?"

Doug nods. "So I guess we'll see you on the Vineyard this summer?"

Ula actually takes my money and counts it. "We'd give you one for free but we told Mable we'd keep track of everything." Ula's mouth is one slim line, like those smiley faces that are supposed to show "in the middle." "So we refuse freebies to everyone."

"That's fine," I say even though it's not and accept the mocha from Doug. "Are these new cups?" I look at the cardboard. It's thinner than the other kind was. "They're not as good—the heat's coming right through." I don't mean to criticize, but heat seepage bugs the hell out of Mable and she doesn't approve of doubling up on cups because of the tree waste.

"They're cheaper," Ula explains.

"Oh," I say. It's really not my business, I figure, and Mable will be back soon and she can sort out the thick and the thin. "Thanks—I have to go. Have a good night."

"Thanks for coming by," Doug says.

"And see you in Edgartown," Ula says. "I'll be helping out there this summer, too."

Oh, fab! Sign me up—sounds awesome. I do a small, not-too-fake smile. Note to self: Complain to Mable about potential for evil twins (okay, so Ula and Doug are not twins; it sounds better) to corrupt café life. Not to mention seriously hinder my Vineyard vibe. But I give a quick wave and manage to get out, "See you then!" before whisking myself back to the safety of my Saab. My Saab that Mable used to drive. My Saab that has already seen me through so many ups, downs, though as of yet no ins and outs. Heh. I press PLAY on the CD again and sing along, *my mind has torn its track to you, my feet can't wait to go* . . . but then my singing fades out while the song continues. With my hands on the steering wheel I approach the dusky campus and realize, unlike how the song finishes, my feet aren't going anywhere. London is over. And I'm back here.

Chapter 3

A few more days of giving into my organizational demons and I've outlined my bio film project that's been approved by PMT and thusly conforms to the very high standards set by the Hadley Hall AC.

"I think it sounds really terrific," Dad says as he crams a whole wheat bagel into his mouth. He got in late last night. I managed to resist the temptation to tuck myself in at nine thirty and heard him pull up (his noisy muffler is a giveaway) much later—like at midnight when I opened one eye to glance at the clock. Of course I also took that time-spotting opportunity to do a quick conversion—if it's midnight here, it's five a.m. in England. I pictured Arabella asleep with her hair spread out on her satin pillowcase, snoring if she's had even one sip of beer, and I pictured Asher. Not that I really know exactly how he looks asleep—not having had the chance to make a deep study of his slumber. But enough to imagine him lying there, peacefully dreaming of me. I hope.

"I hope so," I say and reach for a slice of cantaloupe.

"Here, try this with the melon." Dad slides a pot of yogurt across the table to me.

"I'm fine, Dad."

He looks at me, a little too eager about the dairy products. "Please? It's Greek yogurt with honey in it."

"Oh," I say. "Greek yogurt's big in England. Arabella's mum and dad use it all the time. They even cook chicken in it—it's like a better-for-you sour cream."

Dad's face registers some mark of letdown, as though I've wounded his acidophilus expectations. "Boy—you really learned a lot over there, didn't you?"

Something in his voice sounds different. There's an edge that I've never heard before. Or have rarely heard. I try to place when he's sounded disappointed like this—then it comes to me. When I broke the sacred Hadley Hall parietal rules for sneaking into a dorm past hours. The fact that it was a mistake I regretted instantly doesn't matter—it's still on my record.

"Dad, are you sad about yogurt?" I ask and stare into his eyes, touching his forearm and using a voice from a hemorrhoid commercial. He cracks up.

"No—no. Not about yogurt." He opens his mouth to say something but changes his mind; then he spoons the yogurt onto my melon.

"Dad—I didn't give you PTTMF," I say.

"Fine." Dad swaps my yogurt-oozed melon for an untouched piece. Dad bows his head and asks, "Permission to touch your food?"

"Granted," I say in faux-army speak, then touch his shoulders like he's being knighted—totally mixing my metaphors. Dad slops the stuff on another wedge. I try it.

"Wow—this is so good! Really." I eat every last bit of yogurt and Dad watches. "Dad—you're freaking me out here. Are you obsessed with pushing dairy?"

Dad stands up and clears the table, rinsing the dishes in the sink and putting them in the new dishwasher that he had installed when I was gone. There have been a couple of other slight changes at our house: a new coffee table in the living room, his study is now a library filled with books we had stored in the basement, and there's a whole shelf of organic jams and jellies in the cabinet. "Actually, Louisa made that yogurt." Dad doesn't look at me while he goes on. "She has a piece of property in Vermont—and she has goats there. She's sort of linked up to the local farmers . . ."

"She's a goatherd?" I ask, just because when do you get to ask that question. "Like in *The Sound of Music*?" I go on to do the first few lines from "The Lonely Goatherd" and Dad smiles and turns to me. He stands in front of me, appearing much taller than he normally is (which is pretty tall).

"Love. I like her. I like her a lot." He takes a deep breath, waiting for my reaction.

Without thinking I just say, "That's great, Dad. She sounds really nice. I'm sorry you guys didn't get to visit in London. But let's all meet up soon."

Dad overacts a sigh of relief. "I thought you'd be a little upset—you know, she's my . . . well, I guess she's my girlfriend."

"It's not like she's the first—you dated my math teach for fuck's sake." I immediately wish to retract the swear and I blush, cover my mouth, and try not to laugh nervously.

"Watch your mouth," Dad says without a trace of humor. Cue his headmasterly voice. "You picked up some bad habits in London. Maybe it was considered acceptable to use whatever language you wanted there—but you're back at Hadley now. You're back home."

It doesn't feel like home. Arabella's flat felt like home. I know if I respond to him with that comment we will be stuck in the kitchen arguing, so I don't even try. Instead, I attempt to smooth the moment over with enthusiasm about Louisa. "Well, please tell Louisa that I like the yogurt, even though it comes from a goat. And that I'm psyched to meet her." I stand up and put my dishes in the new machine. "Dad—I'm happy for you. Really."

He gives me a hug and I leave for campus. It's time for me to make a showing.

Of course, just when I decide to bring my body to the greater student body, eschewing my hermit status, I am slammed in the face with a giant poster of Lindsay Parrish.

"I'd like to call her my nemesis," I say to Chris and his yearbook crush-slash-friend, Haverford Pomroy, who are standing next to me, ogling the poster. "But it gives her way too much power."

"Love, you know Haverford, right?" Chris says and gives me a look that tells me to keep the crush factor in check.

"Sure," I say, "Kind of—in that passing nod sort of way."

"Chris speaks highly of you," Haverford says. He's half rugby half surfer, in a faded light and navy blue striped shirt and knee-length shorts.

"I'll try to live up to his description," I say and tie my hair back into a knot. I've been debating cropping it to my chin but feel like I'd enjoy it for a day and then regret it. And the fact that I'm thinking about hair while meeting the guy who's distracted Chris for months makes me a) superficial b) a bad friend or c) both. Behind Haverford is a girl with coffee-colored spirals of hair that radiate from her head, skin the color of milky coffee, and a tight magenta T-shirt.

"And this," Chris says, noticing that I noticed said female, "is Haverford's tragically cool sister, Chilton."

"I'm hardly tragic," she says and shakes my hand, checking me out without trying to hide it.

I think for a second, remembering an email Chris sent me in London. "I thought your name was Chilton David. Not Chilton Pomroy."

Haverford and Chilton overlap each other and try to explain, "Our parents split the names."

"Wait—one at a time, please," I say holding my palms out like the conversation police.

"Okay—so my mom . . . ," Chilton starts.

"Chil—let me," Haverford says and slinks his arm around his sister. Is he gay? Straight? In-between? Chris can't tell, though not for lack of trying to figure it out. Haverford's good-looking and smart and hasn't dated anyone at Hadley since starting here his freshman year, and knows Chris's preference, but so far it hasn't, um, come up in conversation. "So, back when our parents got married they couldn't decide what to do with their names. Very political—who is the head of the house, should we follow male hierarchical history . . ."

"So," Chilton says, "they hyphenated their names— Mitchell David-Pomroy and Davinia David-Pomroy. But then they thought it was too much to say, too much of a burden for their kids."

"So they dropped the David—which was Mom's name," Haverford says. So many people at prep school refer to their parents without the possessive *my*—so it's *Daddy says* or *Mom's the one who* . . . as though they're not your parents.

Chris fills in the rest: "But then their dad felt guilty and their mother felt left out after some grade school parents' night at school, so they dropped Pomroy and just took David."

"This is very involved," I say and make a twisted facial gesture that is supposed to mean something but I don't know what. "So, let me guess, then that didn't work, either, and you all took both and decided to just add and drop at will?"

Chilton nods and adds, "Accurate. Especially because Dad's a filmmaker—you know that, right?"

Right. The biggest African-American filmmaker in the country, if not the world. Yeah, I know that.

Chilton goes on, "Except that taking both names didn't really work very well—because some people know you as one name, other people as the other name so—my advice is, stick with what you've got."

"Advice taken, Chilton," I say and realize I don't even know my mother's maiden name. What an elementary thing—and I don't know it. For security reasons, like when my father gave me an emergency credit card, we just used place of birth and my social security number.

"Mostly people call me Chili," Chilton says. "Chili Pomroy."

"Okay, duly noted." I mime writing down her information and letting my gaze wander to the shiny poster of Lindsay Parrish.

"But when you look us up on the Vineyard this summer, and you will," she says, "we're in the book under David *and* Pomroy."

"And Pomroy-David and David-Pomroy," Haverford adds. "Our parents are a little obsessive."

"They're not the only ones," I say and nudge Chris to re-join the nonfantasy world. He's been gazing at Haverford's shoes as if they could suddenly proclaim their love for him.

"Oh, yeah?" Haverford asks. "What are you obsessed with, Love?"

Chris flinches as if he's been smacked on the shoulder in a rousing game of punch-buggy and I tense up. Did Haverford's voice just sound a little flirty? Did my buddy Chris speak so highly of me to his crush that now the object of the crush has noticed me in *that* way?

I quickly try to stomp out any tension. "I'm trying not to obsess over my boyfriend in London."

Chris gives me the good call look and adds, "They're really in love."

I roll my eyes at him when Haverford's not looking and further disperse the attention by asking, "Hey, Chili, what brings you to our fine institute of learning?"

"I'm coming here next year. I'll be a sophomore." Her bright blue eyes are bright against her skin, which is the color of wet sand. "I've been at Harris."

"Isn't that one of those really tiny places in the Berkshires with . . . ?" I start but she interrupts me.

"Yeah, small, progressive, intense and whacked out. It's a place for future geniuses or tormented artists."

"So why are you leaving?" I ask.

" 'Cause I'm neither a genius nor particularly tormented and it's in the middle of fucking nowhere and I will lose my mind if I go back." She spits all that out fast, and then smiles to show she's over it. "So I handed in all my work to my pod leader—yes, it's called a pod rather than a certain year—and I'm hanging out here until I leave for summer break."

Before I can ask where she's staying, Chris pipes up with, "She's staying in the empty single room at Fruckner. With La Lindsay." Fruckner was filled to capacity but some girl from New York City who was written up in the "Sunday Styles" as "The Club Kid" apparently got a little too much clubbing in and not enough work and was asked to take a leave of academic absence (read: Have fun at public school).

"Oh, lucky you to live in the same house as Lindsay," I say and poke Lindsay's eye with my finger—not the real Lindsay, the poster version. "Let me repeat: She's not so much my enemy as someone I'd love to ignore completely."

"I can see that," Chili says, tugging at her dark hair. "Once you label an enemy, you've sealed your pact with them." She pauses and looks closely at the photo. "Oh my God—she totally had this retouched."

"Where?" Chris is thrilled to be in the know and steps close enough so he could lick the picture of Lindsay.

"Are you going to make out with me?" Lindsay asks as she catwalks by on her way to class. "I thought you weren't interested." She winks at Chris and he blows her a mocking kiss but doesn't say anything back. Haverford watches, and I just can't tell if he was checking out Lindsay's ass or seeing how Chris would react or both. I guess Chris's "is he or isn't he" quest will have to keep going.

"Look—our mom's a commercial photo editor, okay? I know all those tricks. Right here . . ." Chili points to Lindsay's breasts. "She's added shadowing to make them appear—um, larger."

"Like she needed that," Haverford says.

Chris nods. "Not like she was lacking in that department." He looks at Haverford to see if his gaze is boob-bound, but Haverford's backing up to go. "See you guys around—unlike the rest of you, I still have work to finish."

"I have work," Chris says to him. "I'm just choosing to refrain. It's bad for my psyche."

Chili, Chris, and I turn back to the poster.

"And it looks like Lindsay's whole body was digitally lengthened," Chili says. "Maybe I should try that." She laughs and looks at her petite self. She's maybe five feet, but holds herself high so you wouldn't call her tiny. "Just kidding you. I'm in full acceptance of my body." She uses an indistinguishable accent and adds, "We are de lovely womens. Please not for makink body image crisis."

I laugh. "Chris was right about you," I say. "He wrote to me after you visited Hadley this winter."

Chili swats Chris and he pretends to buckle. "What'd you say about me, MLUT?"

"Former MLUT," Chris corrects and blushes. "Nothing. I just told Love that you guys would get along."

The three of us walk to class—or rather, I walk Chris to his Art History class and stand lamely at the doorway. Chili gets ready to head to the tour guide office so she can help lead prospective students and parents around the grounds, one of her "visiting pre-student" responsibilities.

"I almost forgot I'm not a student!" I say and feel kind of guilty, like I'm cutting class.

"Don't question a good thing," Chili says and walks into the room. "And Love—you know I live in Oak Bluffs, right?"

I nod, remembering. "Yeah—you're one town over from me this summer."

She grins and hands Chris's book, Jansen's *History of Art,* to him. "*You're* one town over from *me*—I've been going there way longer."

"Fine—you win," I say and smile at her. "Chris—are you free after this?"

Chris shakes his head. "No—we have an all-school assembly. Wanna come? I'll make lewd remarks and try to make you laugh inappropriately," he promises.

"Maybe," I say and leave him in the dark for art slides while I head out to partake of the activities on the quad.

Lying with my head on my bag and my pale legs stretched out on the newly rolled out lawn, I admire the plants and scenery. Each spring, the grounds crew goes nuts planting and replanting, earthing geraniums and tulips where there was only leftover March mud. All of this outside grandeur is in honor (or honour, if I'm being faux-British) of graduates' weekend when alumni come back for hugs, tours, and hookups with all the people they wish they'd had the guts to approach while actually in high school, and the pinnacle of events: graduation. With tuition rates so high, I guess parents and trustees need to see that the grass really is greener here than anywhere else.

I roll my head to one side to check out the quad action. My buddy from English class, the brainy and ballsy Harriet Walters, is ranting and raving about whatever book she just finished.

"It's a feminist manifesto," she says way too loudly. Given the acoustics of the quad, the sound bounces off the brick walls and people look to see who's killing their springtime buzz.

"Feminist manifesto sounds like a new kind of pasta!" I say and walk over to her.

She hugs me and hands me the book. "You HAVE to read this. Promise?"

"Sure—and welcome back to you, too!" I say. She looks different. Gorgeous, but then she's always been pretty. When you go away from a place and then come back, everyone and everything seem exactly the same and at the same time, totally changed—older, or more together, or more something. Or maybe it's just my view of myself. "No more hair dying?"

Harriet touches the underside of her hair. Where once there was white, or green, magenta and purple, it's now all one shade of light brown. Her librarian glasses have been traded in for wire frames and she's dressed like she's ready for a board meeting, ballerina-prim but not repressed. "I decided that if I'm primarily concerned with people listening to my words, I should let my appearance be plain."

"Well, I like the Amish idea, but quite frankly," I say, studying her up and down, "you look hot."

"I think so, too," Welsh Farrington says and slips his arm around Harriet's waist. Welsh is the best lacrosse player at Hadley and has been since he was a freshman. He's known for his inane comments and his ability to carry heavy objects, and he has the shoulders to prove it. Harriet snuggles into him, betraying the woman unto herself persona she's always had. Welsh notices me over his bulging forearms. "Hey, Love. Haven't seen you in a while. Did you have mono or something?"

"I wasn't sick. I was in London."

"Oh, right," Welsh nods. "Same difference."

Same difference=number three on my annoying phrase list, and I try hard not to say anything. I'm about to comment on how lying in bed with a sore throat, feeling like shit with terrible, debilitating fatigue has nothing in common with gallivanting around London (and while I'm not sure my London life fits the exact definition of gallivanting, it must have come close), and about to ask how long Harriet and Welsh have been an unlikely couple, when I am stopped in my verbal tracks.

I am speechless. Not even capable of miming.

Across the overly green quadrangle, halfway between the heap of book bags and the newly arranged oversized terra-cotta pots containing palm trees (um, hello, we're a New England school—it's not like trustees and alums are going to be swayed into thinking tropical plants really grow here), is the reason for my loss of words.

I back up, away from Harriet and Welsh, who are rather consumed by each other anyway, and duck behind a pine tree. From in between the needles, I watch and am hit again with that breathless feeling that occurs when your past appears in your present.

Standing with his hands in his pockets, kicking at something on the pavement, is Jacob. My Jacob. The boy formerly known as my Jacob but who hasn't been mine for—well—ever, unless you count several magical weeks at the end of sophomore year. He moves toward the student-monikered Stripper Pole, which is of course nothing of the sort, but rather an old flagpole that resides in the very center of the quad (and because the whole campus was designed by a famous mathematician, Lee Rose, we know it's the very center). Jacob slouches down and then sits with his back to the pole and checks out the scene. There's no way he can see me—I'm tucked way into the foliage, but it's unnerving. I have no idea what I'd say, or if we'd talk or hug or ignore each other. By Chris's latest gossip garnish (gossip garnish=that last bit of fluff

on the conversational salad) informs me that Jacob's winter romance with Dillon Fuchs (pronounced Few-ks, though highly
and intentionally mis-emphasized) is over, that it wasn't a big
deal. But who's to say what's a big deal or isn't—how can you
know unless you're in that relationship?

I check my watch—it's two o'clock, nearly time for assembly. Having seen Jacob from a distance, I'm hoping for a close-
up during the all-student meeting. I'm not ready for a
face-to-face, but in the safety of a crowd, I might manage a
better view. It's reassuring to see him sitting by the Stripper's
Pole, though, reading and being his usual observant, calm
self—the guy I knew who played piano by himself and who
wrote Dylan lyrics into his notebooks. Harriet and Welsh
make out in front of everyone. Jacob sits by himself. Some
things change, some stay the same.

Correction: Most things change.

I walk into Fisher Hall, the old auditorium that's used only
for all-school assemblies (not to be confused with all-school
events—those are held all over campus). Assemblies are for big-
time speakers of important historical note, or for Serious Social Situations or issues (SSS—although not to be mistaken for
the mix Arabella made me called SSS=Slow, Sad, and Sadistic,
which was and is brilliant). Fisher Hall is also the place for
Head Monitor elections. Hadley has no mere student body
president, no one governing council. There are lots of positions
like that.

But Head Monitor is the most coveted position because

you have to be voted in doubly—nominated by two faculty
members and then chosen by your peers (read: All the students
who are your friends, lust after you, fear you, or just recognize
your face more than the other candidate's). And, once you're
voted in, you have more power than any other student and
meet with all of the faculty and generally bask in the glory of
your newfound status until you go to college and realize you're
just one of a thousand such people from other prep schools
across the nation. But I digress.

I'm squished into the old-fashioned wooden folding seat
next to Chris and Chili and some of Chris's dorm mates when
Chris gives me a nudge.

"So," he says, raising his eyebrows, "What do you think?"

I stare blankly at him. "Of what?"

"Oh dear—you don't even know, do you?" Chris says. He
puts his palms on my face and twists my head so I can see what
he wants me to see. There, at the front of all the chairs, is a
grand piano.

"So—it's a large instrument they wheeled in. They can
plant palm trees in Massachusetts—anything's possible with the
trustee fund," I say.

"No," Chris shakes his head. "The person playing. You
can't see him from here but it's Jacob."

"My . . ." I stop myself. "Jacob? Really? But he never played
in front of anyone. Well, he played in front of me—and maybe
the coffee house crowd, but he's so shy, he's so quiet, he's so,
like . . ."

"Like about to be Head Monitor?" Chili asks.

Which is exactly what happens. Jacob is called to the stage. More surprising than the fact that he was nominated (teachers have always liked him—he gets great grades and questions their authority just enough so they know he's paying attention but not so much that he undermines it) is the fact of his ease on stage. He waves, smiles, and does those little in jokes with people that makes various members of the student body laugh and cheer. He's like the big man on campus in some movie. Except he's not.

"He's not, right? He was like this person no one else knew," I say to Chris and he tries to shush me. I whisper again. "This is so weird."

"It gets weirder," Chris says and points.

Along with Jacob are two other contenders for the Head Monitor position. At graduation, the current Head Monitor hands over a symbolic Hadley crest that then resides in the monitor's dorm room, proudly on display (read: gathering dust until the next graduation). One nominated student is Betty Yee, and the other is—as it would be in my bizarre world—the leggy, luscious, and lame Lindsay Parrish.

LP is all smiles as she rises from her swampland (aka her seat) and oozes her wrath onto the improvised stage. Like Olympians waiting to have their medals slung over their necks, Lindsay, Betty, and Jacob (cue the violins, cue the sighing—enough so that Chris gives me his *stop* look) stand and accept their verbal praises from the faculty and cheers from the students.

When my father appears, I'm reminded of his split personas. Sure, there's overlap like this morning when his stern tone about my apparently abominable behavior in London— OMG (and other annoying email/IM abbreviations!). But aside from verbal scoldings, I like seeing my father in his authoritative state. He's comfortable in front of crowds; even the student body at large has taken a shine to him. I rarely hear dissent among the troops except when someone's messed up and passes the blame on to my dad, who is usually the nearest high-up upon whom psychological sludge falls. Basically, people like him. He's cool enough, dresses in a manner so as not to encourage immediate ridicule, and has a reputation for being FAIR. Personally, that's one reason I believe he's been quick to enforce rules on me so I can set an example for the entire Hadley campus.

"Okay, settle down." Dad holds up his hand and wrangles us all into silence (actually, I've been silent this whole time save for my sighs). "Thanks to you all for voting—I know it meant making a decision when you were not yet fully awake . . ."

"I missed the election?" I ask Chili.

She nods. "It was this morning before breakfast—if you wanted a say you had to get committed to that ballot box."

So, while I lay in bed wondering what my sweet boyfriend was doing an entire ocean away (drinking coffee with milk no sugar? Buying me my favorite treats at Rococo Chocolates? Or perhaps tonguing Valentine the up-and—dare I say—coming artist?), all the other Hadley students were deciding which person would be at the forefront of my senior class next year.

"I can't believe I didn't vote," I say and stare at the three

candidates. Betty has her hands clasped in front of her, Lindsay
is doing her half smile thing where she looks pretty but is no
doubt brewing her evil thoughts and plans in her mind, and
Jacob . . . Jacob's just—well, I can't go there. Not yet.

"It's not like it was a presidential election," Chris says.
"Plus, you're not even registered—they wouldn't have counted
it."

"True," I say and rest my chin in my hand—the position
Arabella's beauty mag warned is a likely cause of chin acne. But
seeing as chin acne is not, in fact, one of the woes that plagues
me in this life, at least not at this moment, I relish the mopey
pose. "But I would have liked to have known who was
running."

Chris leans forward and puts his head in his chin, too. He
whispers without looking at me. Our heads are nearly touching but we don't look at each other. "Maybe if you got your
head pried out from its perma-place in your ass, you'd be more
aware of the campus goings-on."

"Is *goings-on* one word or two?" I ask him, trying hard to
be annoying. He fights the laughter.

"I just think you've been hiding."

"Wow—you are like so talented in the emotional forensics
department, Chris. I mean, did you get a degree in . . ."

"Oh, shut up. I'm trying to help you." He turns to me and
pretends to peel away layers from my face and shoulders.
"You're like covered with this film of misery and distance."

"Like a character from a Gothic novel," Chili adds.

"Oh, like you even knew me before," I snap at her. "But

yes, you're correct. But we've all got issues and mine have recently overcome my naturally effervescent self. For that, I apologize."

"Apology accepted," Chris says. "Now, is Jacob hot or what?"

I don't—or can't—answer. I just watch in fascination as Lindsay flirts with him on stage, doing the *oops, sorry I touched your thigh with my hand* move, and giggling under her breath. The scary thing is, he doesn't seem offended. Whereas in Mr. Chaucer's English class, the place of our meeting, he always kept away from the shiniest of the moneyed set, the unbearably popular crowd, he now appears to be very chummy with the queen of doom.

So I am most dismayed or surprised or both when my father, unaware of the effect his words will have on me, announces, "This year, we've broken precedent at Hadley Hall!"

An announcement like this always inspires more enthusiasm than is really warranted. When we gained the right to wear flip-flops last spring (prior, shoes had to be "firmly affixed to the feet" as stated in the student handbook) you'd have thought peace had been achieved among dissenting nations. So the students are clapping and whistling now, and my dad continues, "As the years move on, so does tradition have to adapt. In light of this, and in light of the voting count and faculty recommendations, I am pleased to announce the name of the new Head Monitor for next year's senior class . . ." Cue the gasps and ahhs and oohs. "Lindsay Parrish." Cue the mouth open in full disbelief. From me. Cue Lindsay clapping for herself. She'll probably ban nonexclusive fashion labels or make eyeliner mandatory.

Students stretch, ready to go. "But wait—the tradition we're breaking is . . . Lindsay will be spending time with, organizing meetings with, and working late into the evenings with her new Co–Head Monitor, Jacob Coleman. The position is one that requires so much effort; we feel it's best to now have two people, one male and one female, taking care of business."

I'm not the only one to find some sort of innuendo in his words and I watch the stifled laughter around me. Clearly, there's a backstory here and I don't know it.

"Go, JC!" This chant is said many times as seniors and underclassmen alike approach Jacob and pat him on the back. JC? He has a nickname now? Head Monitor is always given to that person whom you expect to win, who has the academics going, but not so much that the studying excludes the social set, and the kicker is that the person's usually really kind. So here we have Lindsay, whose grades are probably fine, and who is a class-A bitch, but popular. And we have Jacob—JC—who up until now had the grades and kind thing, but the über-popular? When did that happen?

"Pretty much right when he came back from Switzerland," Chris explains as we go running together and I ask him. "Look, he was always cute. Then he went away for a summer and a fall and came back after winter break about a foot taller, a bit more broad, and speaking four languages."

"Four?"

"*Si, oui, da, e vero,*" Chris says. "Plus, if you go away for a term at boarding school, when you come back, your stock either rises, as with Jacob. Or plummets, which we see with the not-so-polished Cordelia."

I haven't spoken to Cordelia yet, though I spotted her staring out the front window at her parents' on-campus house (it happens to be attached to my on-campus housing, so it's tough not to be privy to the insider track). Cordelia either didn't notice me or didn't want to, so I took the cue and didn't do the *hey, how's it going* hug, especially since the last time I heard from her was when she helped plot the Lindsay-Jacob connection while I boarded my plane to London.

"Harriet Walters said something about Cordelia going on a vacation to California, to some spa? How'd she swing that?" I jog, pant, and keep up guiding us toward my house. Dad was going to see Mable—alone—today and is supposed to return with a full report.

Chris chuckles and wipes the sweat from his forehead on his blue wristband. "Not so much a spa as a . . . um, how would one say in polite company? A place for healing?"

"Are you saying *spa* is a euphemism for *rehab*?" I ask, slightly shocked. I stop running in front of my porch and start to stretch.

Chris puts his finger to his nose, a very English gesture. "Spot on," he says. "Pleasant Awakenings, I believe it was called. It's supposed to be this alterna-rehab-slash-meditative Zen garden whatnot."

"You know I hate the word *whatnot*," I say automatically.

"I know you do, Love, but I feel it's my duty to challenge your somewhat limited perspectives." Chris gives me a damp kiss on the cheek as a good-bye and I head inside.

As I read through my video manuals and make some notes for my ISPP, I consider the odd feelings I have swirling inside me. So Lindsay has the esteemed position of Head Monitor (um, what position hasn't she had?)—I am so sophomoric, even as a Junior. Then again, Henry Randall and his Vineyard buddies all think I'm finishing Freshman year at Brown.

As if surfing a massive brain wave, I get an IM from LilaL2, aka Lila Lawrence, who seriously did just finish her first year at Brown. With a sinking feeling as I type, I also remember that she had a hot weather hookup during spring break with my best friend's boyfriend.

Luckily, Lila deals with the potential conflict head-on.

LILAL2
Sorry.
LOVEBOO4
About what? Long time no talk, BTW.
LILAL2
My mistake in Nevis.
LOVEBOO4
Oh. Def. unfortunate. But—Toby isn't without blame.
LILAL2
Yeah. He's the one who started it—not that I'm excusing myself.

LOVEBOO4

I think Arabella's okay about it—maybe she was ready
to move on.

LILAL2

I'm done w/classes and heading to Newport after
exams.

LOVEBOO4

Come to MV this summer? Mable's getting better &
plans for café are in full swing. Note: Arabella will be
there, too . . . Maybe you can say sorry in person?

LILAL2

I'm woman enough for that. Gotta run—lots of Euro-
trash to conquer. Just kidding! Oh—almost forgot to
get the scoop on your love life!

LOVEBOO4

Can I take a rain check? I'm all out of love at the
moment.

LILAL2

Sure. But keep me posted re: Hot Henry—he showed
up at a party a while ago and asked about you! More
soon. Xxxxx

I head immediately to my CD stack to find Mable's mix, 100%
Calcium aka The Totally Cheesy Mix. The second song is "All
Out of Love" by Air Supply and I relish the dramarama
melody and OTT lyrics. In the shower, I lather, rinse, and repeat, *I'm all out of love, I'm so lost without you,* and then get the
last of my Daniel Galvin shampoo (Arabella is addicted to her

hairdresser and his products and I see why) in my eyes. My left eye stings. After squeezing out some hair refiner, I condition and for a second wish Arabella were here to talk to (rather than at her present locale which is Bracker's Common at one of her parents' famous and fabulous parties). With wet hair and a green towel that has fraying edges, I decide being at Hadley in this context (i.e., no classes, semifreedom, only the internal pressure from my film project and college essays) isn't so bad. It's kind of like going to summer camp.

Chapter 4

Dressed in spring attire, feeling a certain bounce in my step, I walk to the student center and indulge in a cinnamon bun and ice water so cold it hurts my teeth. Campus looks lovely; the students seem happy and lively. It's the kind of day where everything feels like it's going to work out—Asher will visit, Mable will be healthy, Chris and I will walk the Avon Walk for Breast Cancer and raise tons of money, Lindsay will find herself this summer and return for senior year with newfound respect for others, and we'll all get into the colleges of our choice. Swell.

Of course every lapse into animated pleasantry brings with it a cartoon wolf or witch or gray cloud that hikes you back to the surety that life isn't that easy. I'm relaxing into the too-sweet icing on my pastry, when I find myself immediately reconsidering my thoughts from three seconds earlier.

Jacob Coleman walks through the door with a gaggle of guys. The kind of guys who hook up with girls for sport, with a couple of the sensitive sweet ones dawdling at the sides, and takes a seat on a low couch way off to the far end of the student center.

He's laughing, squished between two long-haired seniors who belong in Hugh Heffner's hot tub. He's doing that laugh that used to be just for me. At least, that's what I thought at the time.

It's like when you love love love a song and are the first to find out about this totally cool band from Iceland or something and everyone thinks you're nuts or doesn't care to listen to your band of choice. You have your special, secret song that's even more amazing because only you and the rest of the Icelandic population know about it. But then suddenly, the Isterflikens (or whatever their name is) get airplay and their single "Volcanic Summer" goes to number one and suddenly everyone knows the band—YOUR indie band. They walk around singing the lyrics out of tune and claiming they knew it a year ago when it wasn't even released. That's how I feel about Jacob. He was just a hottie holding his place well under the Hadley radar when I liked him and now . . .

"Bels, you just won't believe it!" I say and pace around my room. "He's like THE hot guy on campus. How did this happen?"

"See," Arabella says, "you send a boy to Europe for a couple months and you get a man in return."

"Yeah, whatever, you're right—Europe is the heart and soul of culture."

"I miss you," she says and puts on her little girl voice.

"No baby talk! But I miss you tons," I say and frown.

"If I wind up a wrinkled old lady it will be because of you."

"How do you figure?" I ask and look out the window at

the campus from a very safe distance. I bolted from the student center before—I think—Jacob saw me. Not that he would have strutted over to talk or anything, what with his bevy of beauties surrounding him.

"I've noticed I frown more without you around; therefore I am sure to have more lines on my face should you continue living Stateside."

I plop onto my bed and lie down. Then I get a headache, so I sit up. Then I move to my desk chair. "Arghh, I can't get comfortable."

"Because you need to come back," Arabella offers. "I'm sitting in the Bracker's phone booth looking at the front door, just in case you've come to your senses and flown back."

I sigh. "I wish. But I don't. I just started to feel okay, you know?"

"Are you still calculating five hours ahead every time you check your watch?"

"Yes, always," I say. "You know? I think I need to clear my head."

"If I know you, this means either running . . ."

"Done that already." I cut her off and stand up, convinced if there were a pacing Olympics, I could win a medal. Maybe not gold, but bronze.

"Or singing."

"You've got it—I'm heading over to the music rooms so I can belt out Carly Simon at the top of my lungs. I figure if I can sing "I Haven't Got Time for the Pain" at a noise level reserved for showers, I'll feel good as new."

"Sounds like a plan," Arabella says. "I picked that expression up from you, you know."

I nod as though she can really see me. "Before I hang up . . ."

"He's fine," Arabella says. "Not that I've seen much of him since you left, but Asher's okay. He's here, but not here right now."

I picture him in the topiary garden where we first met and swallow my sadness.

"Make sure he visits soon, okay?"

"I'll do my best," Arabella says and blows an overly loud *mwah* kiss into the receiver before hanging up.

The music building is an L-shaped structure well behind the science building and near the faculty parking lot where I used to park back when I first got my license and drove everywhere I could. My trusty car will hold suitcases, my giant duffel bag, some extra kitchen items, and more CDs than I'll ever listen to when I head to Martha's Vineyard for the summer.

When I picture being there in the little cottage in Edgartown, warmth radiates out from my insides. Just imagining waking up there feels good. Even though the place must have baggage for my dad—I mean, it did used to belong to my ever-mysterious mother—for me it feels like home. Arabella and I will have a great time there, and Mable will be our chaperone and we'll all take barefoot walks on the beach and . . .

I stop myself because all of a sudden it feels like I'm reminiscing about things that have yet to occur and that feels depressing. Life should just unfold one day at a time, right?

I settle into the smallest practice room that is still big enough to house a baby grand piano, an ancient music stand, and a chair. It's best to avoid the practice rooms with more furniture or floor space, since those are really where the bored and horny congregate for hookups on Saturday nights.

I take out my *Best of Carly Simon* book of sheet music and start with the first song. I've sung my way from "Let the River Run" to the mind-bogglingly upsetting "That's the Way I've Always Heard It Should Be" to Mable's favorite, "Mockingbird," which I had to skip after the first line because it requires two singers, and I lack my own James Taylor to fill in. Then I proceed, ultraloudly, to do a rendition of "Haven't Got Time for the Pain," which is a classic.

Already, my mood is lifted. Music will always do that for me, just as certain songs will always pull me immediately into memories of places or of certain people. The last song in the book is "You're So Vain."

I start singing and remember that on the Vineyard Mable told me Carly Simon auctioned off the right to know whom she wrote "You're So Vain" about—is it Warren Beatty or James Taylor or Mick Jagger (who sings backup vocals—on the real recording, not in my Hadley Hall practice room. That would be cool, but highly unlikely)? Cooler still to have written a song that makes people so curious even decades later.

You had one eye in the mirror as you watched yourself gavotte . . . I sing it and then wonder out loud what the hell that word means. "Is it a verb? A noun? Both? Can you say I was gavotting past the store the other day and—"

"It's a historical dance term," a voice says from the hallway. The door of my practice cubby is open a crack and I wedge my foot in and open it all the way. Standing there in his trade-marked hands-in-pockets stance is Jacob. "The gavotte became a stylized member of the Baroque dance suite. It was performed after the sarabande."

"Oh," I say and tug on the front of my hair. I don't really have bangs (fringe as Arabella calls it) but there are a few strands at the front that refuse to be held back in a ponytail.

"It was considered a pastoral dance." Jacob nods his head like a chicken, more back and forth than up and down.

"That's really just so much more information than I ever needed to know about the gavotte," I say, my voice totally flat—on purpose both for comedic affect and so I don't let my nervousness show. "But I'm thrilled to know to what Ms. Simon is referring in her song."

"Well, if memory serves, you always did like to know the details," Jacob says and leans on the doorframe. "Then again, it's been a long time."

It's so weird—because part of me feels like no time has passed. We could be back a year ago and he could come into the practice room and kiss me, and it wouldn't seem out of the ordinary. But he's suave now, more casual in his movements. He runs his hand through his dark curls of hair and waits for me to say something.

"Would you like to come in?" I ask and gesture to the tiny room like it's my apartment.

"Don't mind if I do." Jacob sits on the piano bench and I

sit in the rusting metal chair that has been host to many a
Hadley rear over the years.

"So . . . ," I say and hope he interrupts me.

"Yeah," he says. His hands rest on the piano keys and he
presses the white and black notes only halfway, so they don't
make a sound. "Want me to accompany you?"

In life? Um, um, um. Oh, he means sheet music. "Sure. Go
to this one." I stand near him and flip through the pages until
I get to "Legend in Your Own Time." My voice sounds good
on this one; I haven't yet sung it today, and he just might interpret (half falsely, half true) the lyrics pointedly. I get to the
part where I'm supposed to sing *a legend's only a lonely boy when
he goes home alone* and stop. The song is about this guy who
could be Jacob, a quiet guy who found fame. And maybe
Jacob's not in the pages of entertainment mags yet, but he's
certainly building up his campus lore.

"What's wrong?" Jacob asks.

"Nothing," I say. All of sudden I feel like I could sob. Not
just because it's confusing being here with this person I felt so
much for, revealed so much to about my innermost thoughts
and sexual musings, but because of Mable and my dad and my
mother, about whom I am still in the dark, and the whole pas-
sage of time thing that plagues me.

Jacob stands up and turns me so I'm facing him. "You
haven't changed," he says gently and smiles.

"You have," I say and look him right in his bright green
eyes.

He shakes his head. "Not really. Don't think of it as

change—think of it as added life experience." It's a Band-Aid response but one I'm perfectly willing to stick on right now, so much so that when he puts his arms around me and hugs me tightly to his chest (which is without a doubt wider), I hug right back.

"Play something else," I command to break the hug.

He opens the book and begins. *All those crazy nights when I cried myself to sleep, now melodrama never makes me weep anymore . . . ,* I sing loudly, in my best voice (thank you, thank you Carly for your vocal range, which is the closest to mine of any other singer).

Afterward, we don't say anything. I am at a loss for words—can you really just pick up where you left off without a confrontation? And didn't we leave off being a couple? Or do you pick up after the letters we exchanged about losing our virginity or do I ask him about his lascivious past (or present) with Lindsay?

I look at the old-fashioned black-and-white clock above the doorway. "I should go," I say, as though I have an actual appointment somewhere.

"The clock's ten minutes fast," Jacob says.

"Really?" I check it against my watch. "Well, I should still take off."

He stays seated behind the wall of the piano and I collect my music and my bag and nod good-bye.

It's only when I am ensconced in the library that I realize that being in sight of Jacob, both in the music room and when I first saw him on the quad, was the first time I didn't calcu-

late the time change in Europe. I make a mental note to call
Asher as soon as I get back.

"So, that was good," Dad recaps for the fifth time as we enter
the house.

"Yeah—Mable really really seems better, doesn't she?" I say,
not really expecting a response.

Dad sighs and sits down at the table with his new concoc-
tion of Rose's Lime Water and Raspberry seltzer, which I assume is a Louisa influence. He sips and sighs again. "At this
point, I think we have every right to feel hopeful." I smile and
hug his shoulders. "But I do think keeping a sense of reality is
important."

I sit next to him. "Is it okay if I go to the Spring Screen-
ing tonight?"

Dad nods and finishes his drink. "Sure. I appreciate that
you asked."

He's been saying stuff like this lately, like he's proud that I
was "up-front about my whereabouts" when all I did was go
to the supermarket to get eggs (organic, of course). Either he's
just glad to have me back or there's an issue brewing that he's
yet to uncork. It's hard to tell sometimes if I've pissed off my
dad or if he's just disgruntled that I'm getting older, as if it's a
sign we're moving apart.

"What's the film?" Dad asks and tidies the table. Spring
handouts, Mable's medical records, and her medical bills are all
heaped into one stack.

"Oh, we're in luck tonight—it's a double feature. A decent but unlikely pairing of *Grease* and *Jaws*."

"Musicals and monsters," Dad muses. "Wish I could go."

"No, you don't," I say.

"Maybe not," Dad says and I can tell he's distracted by his real plans. He has a great date tonight and plans on taking Louisa for an early evening kayak on the Charles River (my idea) and then further wooing her with wine, cheese, and a gourmet picnic (also my idea, though slightly plagiarized from that last day in London when I was meant to go punting in Oxford or Cambridge, whichever it was. Can it be I'm forgetting already—or no, I probably blocked that last part out?).

I go to my room for a second and then sprint (as much as one can sprint down a spiral staircase without requiring stitches) to the kitchen and hand a sheet of paper to my dad. "I almost forgot—will you sponsor me?"

Dad reviews the words in front of him. "Of course!" He smiles, proud and pleased, and signs his name on my Avon Walk for Breast Cancer form. "If you'd like, I'd be happy to take this to my next staff meeting. It's staff and faculty tomorrow night, so . . ."

"Sure—a little peer pressure's good for fund-raising," I say. "Chris is hitting up the dorm and we thought we'd try to work the dining hall on Sunday night before chapel."

Dad heads to his study and turns on his classical music. Then he reappears. "In case I don't tell you often enough, I love you, Love."

My eyes well up but the tears stay trapped. "Me, too, Dad," I say and then we go our separate ways.

"I'm a little bit Kravitz," Chili says, trying to explain her cultural background as the second film cues up. We already saw an outdated Martha's Vineyard when the film committee screened *Jaws* and now we're all set for *Grease*. From what I've gathered (both from Chris and from watching Chili a little as she finds her footing before officially joining our body of learners next fall), Chili is a girl who manages to float from one crowd and class to another. "My dad's black, my mom's Jewish, and I'm a happy mixture of both. We have bagels and lox at our African-American ancestral house on the Vineyard. What can I say?"

"That you're a spitfire of intellectualism and funk . . . ," Chris suggests.

"With a face that could sink ships?" Chili adds. Then she throws up her hands. "Wait. I meant that in the good way— like I'm so pretty that they'd go off course."

"Don't worry, we got it," I say. "And you don't sound at all full of yourself . . ." We laugh and she displays her face on her hands so we can fake-fawn all over her.

"Here," I say. "Popcorn for all." More than half of the students at Hadley are spread out on the lawn in back of the Science Center. The tall, flat concrete side of the building is where the Spring Screenings are projected, and everyone takes their sleeping bags or sheets and submits to the dewy night. A couple of seniors have pulled their actual mattresses all the way from the dorms, and Jacob, apparently not one to blend in anymore, has thoughtfully erected (ahem) his entire bed, frame and all. He sits in the center of it with a few friends while I am on the damp earth between Chris and Harriet Walters, whose boyfriend, Welsh, is off trying not to get busted for chewing tobacco, which Harriet finds so repulsive that she refused to even walk with him while he dips.

"Question: How sad is it that we're all buzzing at the thought of our curfew extension?" Chris asks.

"Just think—another year from now and we'll be heading to college, where there's no lights-out rule," I say.

"Hey, do you have any pledges for the Avon Walk?" I make my fingers take a fake walk on my hand and Chris adds his to my little mime show.

"Some," he says. "Not as many as I'd like. But I have a scheme to get a whopper of a donation."

"Oh, yeah?"

"Yeah," Chris says and turns his attention back to the big screen. "But I'm keeping it under wraps for right now."

"Okay—well, when you feel like letting me in on your big plans—both the walk and your plans for your so not obviously hidden crush on the nameless one, let me know." I don't say Haverford because Chris hasn't told Chili about his feelings for her brother in case it freaks her out. I think, too, that he's afraid of her finding out and saying his crush is a lost cause.

Chili nods. "I feel your crush-vibe. Come on, what's his name?"

"Never mind."

"Fine—watch the movie," I say, covering for Chris and

wish for a second that life were as simple as singing about your summer boyfriend, flouncing in a poodle skirt, and sipping malteds in a diner. Then Chris pipes up.

"Okay—it's 'Summer Lovin'—we all have to sing," Chris says, and even Harriet Walters agrees. The whole campus erupts in song and for one night, no one is ridiculed, our voices become one, and the world is filled with good old-fashioned harmony.

I lean back on the grass and look up at the muted stars, and feel anchored: to this moment, to this night, to this campus and my friends, to being on this side of the Atlantic.

Chapter 5

The Saturday afternoon mail brings a package with foreign postage stamps. Even though email is easy, there's something so exciting about real mail. I hold the oversized thick cream-colored envelope and wonder if Asher has penned a love missive to me. But the writing on the front is large and loopy and Asher's is formal and small, so I doubt it.

"Anything good there?" Dad asks as he hangs up from his ritualistic phone call to Louisa. "I'm leaving in eight minutes—are you sure you don't want to come?"

"I'm sure," I answer. Dad's thoughtful invite to see Louisa's cottage in Vermont, goats and all, was tempting, but I've decided to pass. It's not that I don't want to meet her or that I have any of those trite *please don't date my daddy* feelings. It's more that I don't want to schlep all the way across New England for one night, hurrying back so Dad can make his faculty meeting on Sunday. Plus, I want to see Mable. "But have fun. Bring me back some cheese."

"Will do," Dad says. "And you know the rules, right?"

"Yep, no overnight guests, all school and dorm rules apply,"

I say in handbook monotone. Dad gives an affinitive nod, then looks at me again.

"What?" I ask.

"Nothing," Dad says, and then thinks better of it and adds, "Just stay you, okay?"

"What does that mean?" I ask.

Dad sighs, then smiles, like he's trying to be upbeat. "I notice—it's that you sometimes give the air of being a chameleon. That you want to fit in with everyone . . ."

I furrow my brow. "Isn't that what teenagers do? Try to fit in?"

"But you're not like that . . ."

"I know, I'm just so special. Look, Dad, I am not the image of conformity you might think I am. I'm kind of different, if you didn't notice."

Dad touches my hair and I recoil, instantly pissed off at him but also guilty for feeling that way. "You think I'm changing in a bad way—but the reality is I'm just growing up and you can't deal with it."

Dad grabs his keys, deposits a peck on my cheek, and says softly, "I know you're getting older. I just want to see you making smart decisions about your life, the people you're with. . . . It does matter."

"I know it matters," I say. "And I'm trying." I don't add the part about needing the space in which to try and fail or try and succeed. It's not that he wants me to be this clichéd little girl or anything; I just think he wants me to be living up to my full potential at all times. I can't doodle; I have to make a piece of art. I can't jot down ideas; I have to write a tome. I can't hang out, because what does that achieve?

I just watch him leave and then look at what the mail brought in: a pretty paper envelope addressed to me.

When I open it, I'm surprised and psyched to find that Nick Adams Cooper has written a thoughtful, interesting, and funny note. Nick Cooper was the only friend of the London titled and entitled set that I really liked.

I'm terribly sorry you had to leave so quickly,

I read and can hear his careful, deep voice.

> *we never got the chance to say good-bye. We never got the chance to really settle in, did we? Regardless, please know that you are in my thoughts as is your aunt. Please accept this donation on behalf of me and my parents—you charmed them completely. Should you ever find yourself back on this side of the Atlantic, please look us up.*
> *Yours,*
> *Nick Cooper*
> *Post Script: Enclosed also find Hemingway's* Nick Adams Stories. *As you are the only other person aside from me who has a literary name, I hope you'll enjoy them.*

Nick Cooper's letter is sweet and caring, and the check enclosed is sizeable, without being tacky. I take the money and the card upstairs and feel funny as I read it again. The book I put on my shelf to read at some point, with Nick's note tucked inside the front cover.

Nick Cooper is the only one of all of the people I met in London who responded to my mass email and Arabella's phone calls about the Avon Walk. Why hasn't Asher written to me? Probably because we've spoken on the phone. But why hasn't he thought to send a card to Mable? Most likely because he's never met her. But Arabella did—she even made a watercolor of her flat and sent it to Mass General (Mable asked one of the doctors to hang it up on the wall so she could dream about foreign travel).

I'm no shrink, but I know enough that maybe I'm not disappointed just in Asher's lack of written words and mention of Mable. Being away from him isn't something I had ever given much thought to while we were together. It wasn't like I walked around holding his hand, contemplating what might or might not become of us as a couple after my program abroad ended. Maybe I was just too busy falling for him in the here and now. And I'm glad I did; it's healthy to live for the moment sometimes. But the trouble is that when you're past that moment, there's not that much left.

I mean, at the end of *Grease* last night I got to thinking: If Danny Zuko and Sandy really had to be separated during the plot scam at the beginning when Sandy says she might have to go back to Australia, would they really have lasted? If Danny had gone to visit her at Christmas (after, I don't know, saving enough money for airfare by drag racing), would they have clicked again? Or was their love circumstantial?

The phone rings and I walk in my movie haze to answer. "Hello?"

"I thought you were coming to visit me!" Mable says.

"I am! I am—I got a slow start." Instant guilt. Mable's probably been waiting for me for ages and I've left my only aunt sitting alone in her hospital room.

"No prob, the coffee twins were here, delivering their most recent anal spreadsheet from Slave. They're really something."

"They seem kind of mean," I say, not editing myself. "At least Ula does."

"Doug's the good cop, she's the bad." I can imagine shaking her scarf-covered head. "But Ula's just trying to set a good example."

"For whom?"

"Oh, are we formal now? For whom is she setting an example? You, probably. They're both going to be sort-of supervising Slave II this summer."

"Oh," my voice comes out small, disappointed.

"Love—you're great and very responsible but let's be real. You're seventeen."

"I'll be eighteen in the fall," I say, pathetically fighting for my maturity.

"Look—it's all set. You and Arabella will be the primary people, okay? You'll open and close in shifts and handle all the press. You can even come up with clever marketing campaigns and everything. I just need Ula to run the books and check in on things." She doesn't say chaperone, but I know that's what she means.

"It's not like I'm a raving party machine, Mable."

"I know, believe me. But it's protocol. I have to have someone of age there just in case." Mable sighs. "Are you angry or will you still visit?"

My shoulders slump. "Of course I'll visit. I just need to let the grumpiness shake off."

"Like dandruff?"

"Yes—just like flaky scalp."

"Gross."

"You're gross."

"Bring me flowers?" Mable asks, hopeful.

"Sure."

"From my favorite place?"

"For you, anything," I say and mean it.

The Flower Market is where the flower dealers get their goods. In the morning, the place is a madhouse with bursts of blooms everywhere. Daring pink dahlias, delicate day lilies, roses in all shades of the color spectrum and petals carpeting the ground. I park between *hell and gone* and *way far away* and carry a straw basket over to the stalls. Most of the crowds are gone, off to sell their wares to the weekend shoppers, but a few vendors remain. I search for lilies of the valley, small slender green stalks with tiny white blossoms hanging off: Mable's favorite flower. They remind me of a story or a song from my childhood, but one I can't remember. I make a mental note to ask Mable about that—sometimes she acts as my memory, retrieving facts I've lost or misplaced.

"Hey, stranger." Harriet Walters sidles up to me, carrying an armful of daisies. "Less than half price." She brags to me about her bargaining prowess and sticks a white daisy behind my ear. "You're a vision of near summer."

"Thanks," I say and put my basket down for a second to take off my sweater and tie it around my waist. "I'm so hot—I can't believe it's this late in the school year."

"I know. Almost senior year." Harriet doesn't say anything else, but I gather from her facial expression that she's thinking what I am—where will I be at the start of senior year? What will have changed? Or will everything have stayed the same?

"Are you going to college?" Harriet asks. She managed to sound so focused all the time, not overly academic, just like she's thoughtful and careful about her words.

"Of course I am, why?" I furrow my brow and try to block the sun by using my hand like a visor.

"I don't mean it as an insult," Harriet qualifies.

"No—I know. It's just like that's the ultimate sin or sign of prep dissention, right? Not going to college when prep school was created to *prepare* you for the rigors of university life." I take the flower out from behind my ear and absentmindedly start plucking the petals.

"People are afraid to stray from their life plans—maybe they think if they take a step off the path they won't find their way back, you know?"

I pause, considering what she said. "You're a smart person, Harriet."

She tilts her head, smiling. "Thanks. I'll leave you to your wisteria wandering."

"Not wisteria—lily of the valley."

"Try five stalls back over to the left," she says and walks away.

I mull over what she said—not that I won't go to college. I have every intention of enrolling and enjoying myself and learning and all that. But what about pausing—or not so much pausing since that implies stagnating—but taking a break from all the crazy pressures and classes? Maybe I would benefit from a year off, like so many people do in England. They even have a term there—year out. She's on her year out, they'd say about me. But you can't just sit there on your year out; you have to travel or volunteer or get a job, which leads me back to what do I *want* to do?

At the stall, I find just enough lilies to make a bouquet for Mable. I hold the flowers gently, as if they are her bruised and cold hand, and head to the hospital.

Mable's whole face lights up when she sees me. "You found them! My favorites!" She takes the flowers from me and sticks them in the pink plastic water pitcher that rests on the rolling cart near her bed.

"The last ones," I say. Today is a special day since Mable is well enough to sit at the chair by the large window in her room. The view is the Boston skyline, and we sit admiring the

sunny day, enjoying just being together until I remember my
mental note. "Hey—what memory am I blanking on with lily
of the valley?"

Mable frowns. "I'm not sure," she says.

"Yes, you are," I say and lean across the small round table so
I'm closer to her. "When I was little. There was a book or a
song—way underneath useless factoids in my head. I have a
special attachment to these flowers. Not just because they're
your favorite."

Mable turns away from me and stares out the window
again. I wonder if she's wishing she were well enough to be out
there or if she's looking at a certain landmark—Fenway Park,
the flashing Citgo sign—and remembering something she
doesn't want to share. "I don't know what you mean. I can't
remember, either," she says but her tone is one I know well. It's
the tone she uses only when I ask about my missing mother,
or my parents pre-me. Early days. The mystery of it all. Usually she warns me away from these topics, but this time, I'm
undeterred.

"Mable, come on," I say.

"Oh, Love . . . ," she sighs and adjusts in her seat.

I go and crouch next to her, my hands on her knees. "Some
day, I'm going to know. All of it. Or if not all of the past, then
most of it."

"Some day isn't now," Mable says quietly.

"I think it is," I say.

"I want to go back to my bed," Mable says. "Call the
nurse."

I obey her command and pull the help cord by her bed and ask for help. While Mable sits in the chair, sunlight streaming in the glass, the rays illuminate her, making her glow. I sit on her bed, staring at the watercolor of Arabella's flat. The painting is titled "Arabella (and Love's) Flat, February."

"It was a song," Mable says finally. I don't even look at her in case she stops talking. *White choral bells upon a slender stalk, lilies of the valley deck my garden walk.* She sings the last few words and my eyes fill up immediately with tears. But not about her—not about anything I know—some very odd, empty sad feeling.

She goes on, "There's more, about wishing you could hear the flowers ring."

"Oh wait—that just gave me a really weird feeling—I remember thinking that the blossoms really could ring. That they were a fairy flower or something magical."

Mable looks at the flowers. "They are, kind of, aren't they?" I nod. "Your mother sang that song to you."

"When I was a baby?" I cannot fight my intense curiosity.

"Then—and a bit after . . ."

I close my eyes and rest my face in my palms. Hearing about the years before I knew how to know makes me tired. "When you sang that song, it made me think of a blanket—at least I think it's a blanket—we had a long, really long time ago." I open my eyes to describe my mental visual. "It was navy blue, with a sort of viney pattern on it, roses or—no morning glory—on it. I wonder what happened to that blanket."

Mable looks at me and the nurse comes in to help bring

her back to bed. "That I can't tell you—really, I'm not hiding it—I have no idea what happened to that jacket."

"Jacket? I thought I said blanket."

Mable moves slowly, holding on to the nurse for support. She's supposedly better but still seems so weak. She slides under the stiff hospital sheets and says, "You did. But it wasn't a blanket. It was a jacket. That much I know."

"I think she needs to rest now," the nurse says and Mable gives a small nod.

I give her a kiss and walk to the door. Then I go to the flowers, move them closer to her so she can see them when she wakes up, and take one stalk for myself. It smells like spring: new and sweet and filled with longing.

Dad comes back early, claiming Louisa has an upper respiratory infection, but I get the feeling there's more to his speedy return than just a hacking cough and a fever.

"Squash?" Dad asks.

I pretend not to know what he's asking. "Noun: a root vegetable."

"Very funny," he says. "Want to play?"

I shake my head. "Can I bow out today? I'm tired. I went to see Mable yesterday and worked this whole morning on my video project. I start filming her this week, and I had to get the whole documentary formatting done."

"I'm sure it'll be an interesting project. What about all your other papers?"

I smear some Labello on my lips, thankful I still have

enough of the Euro-Chapstick to last me until Arabella brings restocks this summer. "Two I've completed, one is nearly done, and the other is a 'creative component' that has yet to be announced—at least to me. Poppy Massa-Tonclair is sending an email to me this week about it."

Dad nods as though he's checked off another item on his forever-multiplying list of "things to do." He stands waiting for me to say something, bouncing his squash racket off his knee.

"Want to come see a place I like to hang out?" I ask, suddenly feeling like I haven't just relaxed with my dad since I got back. Which would really mean in months if you add up the time I was away.

"Will I like this place?" Dad asks.

"It's not a bar, not a strip club, not a . . ."

"Oh, quick, shield my eyes!" Dad makes a face, dubious. "I don't know, Love . . ."

I poke him in the shoulder in indignation. "Dad? Come on—it's not like I'm a wild child."

Dad tilts his head side to side as though he's considering my choice of names for myself. "You didn't used to be."

Then I see that Dad's only partially kidding. "You see kids every day who have issues. Big-time issues. Then look at me." I stand in front of him dramatically so he can see me. "And I'm not like that."

"No," Dad agrees, his voice quiet. "You're not. But you're not the same, either."

I don't know what to say to this, so I say nothing. I just pull him by the sleeve like I used to do as a child when I wanted to change locations at the playground—and lead him to where I want to go.

In light of my inappropriate jesting about my "hang out" place, Dad is thrilled beyond words to find that the place to which I was referring is the pole vaulting mat.

"What's so great about this place?" he asks as we stand at the edge of the thick, blue cushion.

"Come on—can't you see the intrinsic value?"

"I'm too old," Dad says.

"Your loss, then," I say, knowing Dad will follow me. I take a running jump and do a silly snow angel in midair form leap, and land on my back, protected by the mat. Dad pauses, then does the same, landing on his back, upside from me and laughing. We lie there for a minute laughing, and then look up at the blue sky.

"Another year," Dad says, still looking skyward.

My head is almost touching his head, and I reach up so I can take his hand. We watch the clouds move, shouting out their shapes like we did when I was a kid.

"A thimble!" he says.

"A unicorn!" I point and then blush—maybe I'm still a fifth grade girl if I'm still seeing flying horses in the sky. Then flying horses makes me think of the antique carousel on Martha's Vineyard.

"The state of Idaho," Dad says.

"Am I lame that I don't even know what that looks like?" I ask. "Oh—hey—there's a turtle with a top hat!"

"Oh, I see that!" Dad says and we're both very excited that we see the same cloud images. We pause for a minute. "I'm not sure what's going to happen with Mable."

I don't move or try to get a look at Dad's face because I can tell he's crying. "You mean you don't know if she's really better? I thought you just said we should be hopeful."

"Better is a loaded word, Love."

"So what're you saying?" I squeeze his hand and wish we could go back to looking for thimbles or unicorns or Ferris wheels in the sky.

"I'm saying let's really enjoy what we have now," he says and sobs hard enough that the mat shakes underneath us. After being quiet for a minute, the feelings start to overtake me and I cry, too. It's so sad to see or hear a parent cry, especially when you feel the same sadness they do. It's like the person who is supposed to reassure me can't and we both know it.

We stay like that for a few minutes until we've both gotten the tears out of our systems for now.

"Here," Dad says as we sit up. He hands me a granola bar.

"Do you always travel with food?" I ask, my voice still shaky from the cryfest. I accept his oaty handout.

"Actually, I do," he says. "It's an old habit. Once, your . . ." He pauses. "Once I was on a road trip and ran out of gas and had to walk nearly ten miles to a station. What bugged me most wasn't the walk; I—I had good company. But I was so hungry. Since then I always carry a little snack with me. Even just a tiny thing . . ."

"So that's one of your life lessons to hand down? Always

bring food?" I smile. First, Dad nods; then he thinks of something and his face changes. "What?"

"Nothing—it's not the time."

"Dad—if there's an issue or whatever, you should tell me.
I mean, I know we're having father-daughter time here but
just say it." I nudge him with my toe. "I know you've had
something bothering you since I got back, you might as well
tell me." I've noticed that Dad's been stopping himself from
saying something—completing a thought during some of our
discussions. Like right before we came to the track, he was on
the verge of letting me in—but then he stopped.

We reposition ourselves so that Dad is in the center of the
mat, his long legs stretched out in front of him. He sits up
looking at me while I sit on the edge of the mat with my legs
dangling off, feet resting on the sandy grass below. It probably
looks like I'm trying to escape.

"Is there anything about which you feel you haven't been
up front with me?" Dad asks.

"I hate questions like this," I say. The wind picks up; it's one
of those soft presummer breezes that call to mind the beach,
not the running track in the midst of a confrontation. I wish I
were already on the Vineyard. With Arabella. Or just Mable. Or
just by myself. I could be doing that "moody girl on a beach
with a journal" thing, scripting songs and enjoying the dunes.
Briefly I indulge my vision—somehow I'm in jeans but not
too hot, or in shorts but not getting burned and my pen is fluid
on the page. And then in the distance, a boy . . . but I can't
make out who it is—Asher? Nice posh Henry? Or that other

Vineyard boy, Charlie. Boat Boy Charlie who might be penni-less but certainly is endowed with many a stunning trait—ditching me at dinner notwithstanding.

"Are you even listening to anything I'm saying?" Dad moves closer. "I'm trying here, Love, I really am. But it's very frustrating when you won't communicate."

"Sorry, Dad, I tuned out for a minute."

"You tuned out a long time ago," Dad says. "You used to share so much with me . . ."

"I still do—you have no idea how much I tell you com-pared with other people. Do you think Chris is on the phone telling his mother his innermost thoughts? Come on, Dad, at least be fair. As far as teenage-parental conversing goes, you get a lot from me. We're as close as we can be."

"And I hope you get a lot from me, too," Dad says sound-ing wounded.

"Plus, it's not like you've been around all the time. You have Louisa and that's great, but you can't expect me to talk to you when you're off doing goaty things."

Dad nods. Maybe I'm not in trouble. He just wanted a heart to heart. "We're getting off track here."

"I'm on the track," I say and point to my feet that are grounded on the running track. Dad smirks but doesn't offer me a full smile. Maybe my feet aren't the only things that will be grounded—though for the life of me I can't figure out what trouble I'm in—it's just a feeling.

"When I spoke about being up front I meant before now—this past term."

"You mean when I was away?" I look at my hands. I'm surprised to find my fingers shaking slightly.

"Yes." Dad doesn't elaborate. It's one of his head principal tricks that he does to get people to talk—the more he lets students ramble, the more likely they are to admit to doing something they shouldn't.

"No, I don't think so," I say. Of course I realize I'm lying and that maybe Dad knows this. So I offer up a little admission so that he'll know I'm trying. "People drink sometimes there—they do here, too, and I'm sure you know about that what with Lindsay Parrish's blood alcohol level on high alert last fall . . ."

"This isn't about Lindsay Parrish."

Of course I know this but I'm trying to divert the attention by bringing up anything it could be before he explodes. "And yes, you were right before—Arabella swears all the time—it's just her thing and I picked it up and I'll try not to."

"I don't really care about the swearing. I'm sure you'll figure out how to speak appropriately."

"I had some wine," I admit.

"I figured as much," Dad says. I wait for him to ask something such as did I get in a car with someone who'd been drinking or if I had sex—oh my God, this is about sex. My dad wants to know if I had sex.

I blush and stammer, then regain my composure. "I know about condoms," I say.

Dad wrinkles his brow. "Great. Good for you."

Oops, wrong answer. "Is this about sex?"

Dad sighs. "Ah, no." Then he reconsiders. "Unless you want to talk about sex—you know you always can with me— or with Mable and you know how important those decisions are. Once you do something, you can't take it back . . ."

"I get it, Dad. Sex is not like an exchange at The Gap."

Dad coughs and scoots over so that he's sitting next to me. "I'll be very blunt now so we can save any further guessing at your wrongdoing . . ."

"So I did do something wrong?"

"You sure did," Dad says. "When you signed off for a term to LADAM you were under strict orders to act under their jurisdiction."

I hold my hands up, confused. "I did . . ."

"You went to class as commanded, adhered to the rules set by that administration . . ."

"Yes," I say, my voice adamant (not to be confused with Adam Ant, a rock star from the eighties who once signed Mable's bare midriff—tasty!).

"And as part of this you lived at the LADAM dorms?" Dad stares at me, eyebrows in fully raised, antibullshit position.

"Yeah," I say. Mostly. For that first part.

"I spoke with Angus Piece . . ."

"You called Arabella's parents? Why?"

"I was in the process of making arrangements for Arabella's flight over here," Dad starts. "But when he casually mentioned that she was at her flat packing up the last of your things, it dawned on me that you hadn't complained about the dorm conditions in a long time. Plus, it puts into context the watercolor in Mable's hospital room. What's the title? Arabella and Love's flat?" Dad sighs out his nose.

"Dad—okay." I take a huge breath like I'm about to plunge under water to find something I dropped—oh, yeah, my summer plans! "I messed up—clearly I was supposed to stay in the dorms. And I did. For a long time and then it was just gross. I mean people were barfing outside my door and wandering in at all hours of the night—the noise was intolerable."

"I would have complained for you," Dad says. "Gotten you another room there."

"It wouldn't have accomplished anything! It's just how it is there, in all the rooms. So Fizzy and Keena . . ."

"Your friends," Dad says.

"Right my friends . . ."

"Who still lived in the dorms despite the squalid conditions? And Keena is Poppy Massa-Tonclair's daughter, a faculty brat who still managed to cope?"

Chris jogs by and gives a friendly wave and what's up and I shoo him away with a frantic flailing of hands. He shrugs and keeps going.

"Arabella had a flat, Dad. It's this incredible place—and her parents, who were my in loco parentis, in case you've forgotten, said it was okay."

"The Pieces—Angus and Monti—are hardly conventional people—they do not set the bar on parenting as far as I'm concerned. And they never cleared it with me. They never signed papers. There are rules to which you must adhere."

I stand up and look at my dad. My hands are on my hips,

my hair blowing into my face, making me scratch my cheeks. "You don't get it! It was just different there, Dad—and believe me I got into no worse trouble at her flat than I would've at the dorms."

Dad sighs. "I know. I've thought about this a lot, Love. That's why it's taken me so long to confront you."

"So you've been plotting my demise this whole time?"

"I've been doing no such thing. You were in charge of yourself in London. You have only yourself to blame." Dad stands up and we stand next to each other, looking at the blue squishy mat like it's a mess we have to clean up. "I'm upset you didn't tell me over the phone from there. One lie breeds another—you didn't tell me your living situation; you went behind my back, which puts Angus and Monti in a situation of great liability . . ."

"I'm sorry," I say. And I am. I don't want this to be some legal battle or long-standing issue, but I'd do it again. I loved that flat and I loved living on my own, away from all the noise and rules.

"But what I'm mainly concerned about is that despite our seemingly close relationship—the one you just described as being 'as close as can be'—you felt okay about belittling all that trust. I understand poor living conditions—I did spend a semester in India."

"You did?" This is news to me. "When?"

"Never mind—the point is—no matter how bad you wanted to get out of those dorms, you weren't supposed to. But you completely went against the rules."

"I wish you could just have seen me there—seen my life there."

"Obviously, I wish that, too. You've grown tremendously, Love, and that's a powerful, wonderful thing. But with growth comes responsibility. And I'm not sure you understand that aspect . . ."

He starts walking back toward our house and I follow. The tension lifts a little as we leave the track behind, but I sense there's more. I'm tired of waiting for the worst so I ask, "So what's the deal with this, then? Am I grounded?"

Dad scratches his head. His hair has started to thin at the top and it dawns on me that one day he'll be old and bald and I'll be his age. It makes me want to hold his hand and savor every minute with him, but then I'm thrust back into the situation I'm in now and think, who holds the hand of the person who's about to inflict punishment?

"Not grounded—that's not fitting." He mumbles some classical music, one of his "I'm thinking" habits. We reach the front porch of the house. "I'm not sure what the ramifications of this will be. Because you weren't a Hadley student at the time, this doesn't go through their committees. It's just a family issue—and one I need to think about more."

"So what am I supposed to do in the meantime?" I ask.

"Do as Bob Dylan said—keep on keeping on," Dad says and smiles, trying to show me it's time to drop it and lighten up. Easy for him to say.

"Fine." I let him go inside and I sit in one of the wicker chairs on the porch. Maybe he'll make me write an essay about how I acted. Or maybe he'll take away my campus privileges and make me stay in my room—fine with me. He wouldn't cancel the Avon Walk; I haven't mentioned any parties (although he surely is aware of the traditional Crescent Beach bash after graduation), so he can't cancel those plans . . . but then suddenly it occurs to me that he has every power to veto my Vineyard plans and change my summer altogether.

Chapter 6

"It's good to see you," I say to Jacob. He sits across from me in an oversized brown leather chair, looking casual and cool, and somehow not at all overheated despite the fact that it's ninety degrees outside.

"You, too," he says.

This could be the opening lines of a date—except that we're not on one and we are, in fact, waiting for our separate (but equal, of course) appointments with the college counseling office. As with so many infallible electronic programs, it turns out the SIBOF is fallible and has proven it this week by the counseling office's memo:

> Dear _____ (insert names of one third of the junior class):
> We regret to inform you that the SIBOF scores issued to you last term might have been incorrectly weighted. Please return to the CCO by the end of the day to receive your reissued scores.

Jacob and I seem to have come at the last possible second—the office has had a line out the door snaking all the way past Maus Hall (aka Eek!) and heading to the Arts Dome all day. Now though, the office is fairly quiet, save for the buzz of the infallible/fallible computers and the phones that won't stop ringing (parents are most perturbed by this news: What if Biffy/Jenkins/Lucy doesn't really have a shot at Harvard/Yale/NYU? Gasp!).

"So, where are you going, anyway?" Jacob asks. "Some music school?"

"Maybe," I say. "Actually, you know what? I don't have a clue." I laugh at myself in disbelief. Everyone here is so focused, so poised, and positively determined to get to the ONE top choice school that I am relegated to freak status for not matching their determination. "I mean, don't get me wrong. I want to go to a great school, one that makes sense for me . . ."

"So you don't care about the cachet of the Ivies or anything?"

"I never said that. All I know is that it's more important to me to find a place where I really want to go than it is to get into a school just because it's ranked number one in the country."

"I take it your SIBOF was incorrect?"

I nod. "Yours?"

Jacob says, "No—I never got my list of reach schools and safeties . . . I was in Switzerland."

I roll my eyes at him—I can't help it. Cue the monotone voice: "I know where you were." I mean, I wrote to you there, for God's sake.

"Oh, yeah, I guess so . . ."

To cover a potentially miserable what–the–hell–happened scene, I continue with the college conversation. "Any thoughts on your destination after Hadley?"

Jacob shrugs. Thoughts on the school of shrugs related to people asking if you've thought about college include: the single-shoulder shrug: *I'm not about to launch into this now. I know exactly where I want to go and I'm so desperate to get in that I won't chance jinxing it by saying it out loud and if I don't get in I will transfer in after freshman year at some state school and then pretend that freshman year never happened.* The double kind of shrug and tight smile combo, which is typical Hadley Hall. It's overtly casual, like *Oh, hey, college—what a good idea, I might just check out that scene—my dad was fifth generation Harvard, maybe I'll take a look there—gotta make sure it's the right fit for me, you know?* Then there's the ever-popular "coy meets self-effacing double-shrug and eyebrows raised," which translates to *Of course I've thought about college and more than likely I've already written my essays and have a grand life plan, but I'll shrug anyway to look spontaneous and hopeful.*

"What kind of shrug was that?" I ask Jacob, assuming he knows the types.

"The not really sure if I'm headed to college right away; I'm not particularly focused on that as my life's ambition." He bites at his lip and flips his hair out of his eyes. "I'm full of shit of course."

"How so?"

"How so . . . um, because on the one hand I don't want to

be like everyone else and like my dad who wants me to go to Stanford so badly that he won't mention the name. Like not bringing it up as a potential place will make me more inclined to choose it. But on the other hand, it matters to me—sure. I work hard to get good grades and I want my college to reflect that."

"That sounds like a line you memorized for a college interview," I say and think about poking him in the ribs, but then decide it's too familiar, even though I've been so familiar as to put my hand on his ass when he kissed me. But I digress.

"It is—well, spotted. When I was abroad I just kind of dropped out of the whole race. I have every intention of going to a great university but I'm not going to let that quest define me for the next year plus."

I so know what he means. Being in London put so much into perspective—and yet, being back here, it's hard to keep that outlook. "I think I just need to look around more—go visit some places and get a sense of what it'd be like to *be* there."

"Yeah, I agree. I'm headed for a big-time road trip this summer." He reflects for a minute. "The route I've planned is not particularly gas-efficient but it affords a certain nationwide view."

"I have to tour, too," I say, "but I'm also working on the Vineyard." At least, I hope I'm still doing that—but who knows—maybe Dad will have planned for me to sheer goats at Louisa's as penance.

"Cool," he says but doesn't ask me to elaborate. Therefore

I don't have to choose between edited versions of my story—the one where it's just me and Arabella, two hot girls alone in a cottage feel free to visit, etc. Then there's my titled gorgeous English boyfriend—oh, haven't I mentioned him?—is coming to visit. Or I could really up the ante (note to self: Learn poker so using this expression is validated by actual knowledge of ante-in) with the well, I have to see what happens with all those beautiful Vineyard boys . . . or just the real answer, which is that I'm running the café, writing songs I won't perform, and hanging out with my best friend, contemplating all of the above.

"How much longer will we have to wait?" I ask and drum my fingers on my thighs.

"Am I boring you that badly?" Jacob looks away from me and switches positions so he's leaning over the little table between us.

"On a scale of one to ten . . . ?"

"Don't answer that," Jacob says and thumbs through one of the ancient catalogs on the round oak table. All the recent college literature gets "borrowed" by interested Hadley students, so what remains at this time of year is stuff from the old files. "Here—this is you, lunching with your buddies at the cafeteria." Jacob points to a horribly outdated photo of some girl with greasy, flat red hair (granted it's a somewhat similar hue to mine, though I cannot claim the sheer oil content that she can).

"Oh, right! Gertrude and Beth, I met them at a peace rally," I say. "Gertie's really talented—she made her outfit entirely from discarded tube socks. And Beth—well, she's been around the block once or twice but she can sure bake a mean blueberry cobbler." I flip through his catalog, then grab one for myself and randomly open it. "I didn't know you were theatrical!" I point to a guy in a unitard, his face contorted (possibly from the pain of the unitard).

"I was found by a scout—plays are my life now," he says, then points to a curly haired student giving a tour. "That and doing nature walks on campus. I found my calling."

We're quiet for a second, tucking the laughter in, until I find another picture: This time it's clearly from the fifties—the female has her hair in a ponytail, her crisp white blouse is tucked into her high-waisted skirt. Next to her is a guy so clean and ironed you could cut vegetables on his back. The picture is photographed from behind. "Hey, look, it's us . . ." I start but then cut myself off. It's not a funny photo—it's sweet. It's that beginning stage of love captured so clearly, so sweetly that it transcends time.

"Change the fabric and it could be now," Jacob says and touches the picture right where the sun is sinking.

"I guess some images are timeless," I say and close the book.

We sit there, in half silence (it can't qualify as total silence because Mrs. Dandy-Patinko, with uncharacteristic vehemence, yells into the phone that she is not personally responsible for the statistical error and that she is sure all the students will get in somewhere, even if it's not their first choice of school. This is the academic equivalent of telling a parent to shut up).

Then Jacob turns to me. "Want to hang out some time?"

It's not suggestive, not overfriendly, not flirty—just nice. "Yes, I would," I say and then it's my turn to go in and find out what my future holds.

Six hours, four trips to the bathroom, two lattes, and a movie-sized box of Raisinets later, I am less on my way to figuring out what to do for PMT's final project than I'd hoped to be. Aside from my ISPP, which is half Hadley, half LADAM credit, I received word from Poppy Massa-Tonclair that all of her students were meant to submit "significant works of literary merit." When I emailed back asking for examples, she cited such ideas as the first half of a novel, a longer-length novella, a complete book of poetry, an anthology of essays related to the quest for self, *An Oral History of Family: Ten Hours of Verbal Documentary,* and so on. Oh, right, I have that here in my back pocket.

Of course, Jacob wrote a novella last semester for extra credit—and I thought about asking for the privilege of reading it, but I figure that if he wanted me to, he'd offer. Plus, even though it's fiction, I'm semihesitant to find traces of truth in there.

The ideas I've been working on for my own project might not pass muster (when I was little I thought that phrase was "might not pass mustard." Yes, Love, condiments are forever appearing in common language). Nothing has really jumped out at me. Could I submit a book of songs? Sure—but then I'd have to finish all of them and some are better than others (read:

Some suck and some are decent). Plus, it doesn't feel like enough. The project is meant to convey an aspect of ourselves we have "yet to bring to the table," so until I find out what— or whom—I've yet to dine with, I'm doomed to obsess.

I head back to the house in time to have a surprise first meeting with my dad's new (to me) girlfriend. Had I not had a good description of her (tall, athletic build with wavy dark hair and a sort-of beaky nose—her words, Dad insisted, not his), I would have thought she was trying to break into our house.

"Louisa? Is that you?" I ask and take the few stairs up to the porch in one big leap to save her from further pounding on the door. I reach out my hand to shake hers and she grips mine.

"Oh, Love! Hi!" She smiles at me and seems a little embarrassed to be caught in midknock. "I was supposed to meet your father here but I couldn't remember what time, and now I think I've missed him and . . ."

This first meeting should feel weird or forced, but it doesn't. I guess I've heard so much about her it's as though I already know her, even though I don't. And probably, she feels the same thing about me.

"I think my dad's in a meeting," I say, and it could be true—it's usually true or else he's playing squash or having lunch, which is essentially a meeting but with food.

"Oh." She looks genuinely disappointed. "Well, I'm happy to meet you—finally!"

We stand on the porch making chitchat for a bit, and then

it occurs to me that my dad would like it if Louisa and I could be friends. Feeling very mature, and noticing that she's in full-on exercise gear, I ask, "Would you like to play squash?"

Louisa smiles like I've asked her to the prom, but probably she's way more nervous than I am since her status with my dad is more precarious. "Oh, you're sweet to offer—I know it's not your favorite. I was going to play squash with David, not that I know how, but he's . . . of course you already know this . . . a very enthusiastic player and since I showed him how to shear a sheep . . ."

"My dad sheared a sheep?" I ask and crack up. She's easy to be around, and pretty in that softer, older way—not a hottie like Mable—but gently attractive.

"He helped to shear one, yes," Louisa says. "It was more like, 'Now, lamb, listen to me . . . ' He tried to reason with the animal." She watches me laugh and adds, "Don't worry—I took pictures."

Then there's that post-laughter quiet in which we both stare at each other. I'm thinking, okay, so here's the woman my dad really likes—loves, probably—and maybe she's thinking, so here's the girl I've heard so much about, and the only thing we really have in common is the man who isn't here. The one who's in a meeting.

"Your dad mentioned that you like to run," Louisa says. She doesn't come right out and suggest anything, but I'm sure my dad would be thrilled if the two women in his life (three if you count Mable) went running and got chummy. Or at least got in a cardio workout together.

"I do—I could show you the trails behind the dorms . . ."

"Fantastic!" she says.

"Let me get changed," I say and unlock the door so I can put on shorts and a T-shirt. I suspect that getting to know Louisa will be like wearing a T-shirt—bright and new at first and then, before you know it, comfortable and faded like my Hadley running shorts that were so stiff at first and now are fraying at the edges.

"That's enough about college," I say to Mable and stand up to try to shake off the talk of essays, classes, majors, grades, and summer tours. "Jacob had a good thing . . . How'd he describe it? That he wants to go to a great school but he's not going to . . ."

"Jacob?" Mable clears her throat in dramatic fashion and commands that I sit down again. We're in our spot in her hospital room. She's been spending more and more time out of bed, taking walks in the hallways, and even getting to sit outside every day. "You'll need to backtrack—I need all the details."

I shake my head. I've gone through it so much in my own journal, my overanalyzing brain and with Arabella and Chris that I can't explain it. "I don't know. There's nothing going on there . . . He's back, I'm back, and we're back in touch. We haven't dealt with anything."

"You never discussed your letters or talked about Lindsay?"

"No, not Lindsay, not any of his other—people," I say, unable to get my mouth to form the word *girlfriend,* and put my hand to the window. I don't even add in that there were other hookups, presumably, Swiss maidens or foreign future princesses while he was aboard, the fact that he officially became a campus couple with Dillon Fuchs, one of those girls who is the subject of much lust but always seems to be too sophisticated to date people at school. My palm leaves a mark that stays for a few seconds, then fades like a crush. "And the thing is, I don't really want to."

"Because you live in a dreamworld, Love," Mable says. Maybe she meant it as a joke but her voice sounds weary, which gives her statement a validity I find hard to take.

"What do you mean?"

"I mean, you don't always look at things for how they really are. You choose to accept a situation at face value rather than looking deeper, exploring what you feel and what's really there. You'd rather fantasize about the prospect of something than do it."

I press PAUSE on my video camera. It's been on the last few times I visited, and once when my father came at night with the doctor's permission to film Mable as she slept, just so I'd have the footage.

"Don't turn it off now—that's what I'm saying—capture all of this," Mable says and rises up to press RECORD again.

"This project is about you," I say. "Remember?"

"Right," Mable says.

I look at my hands in my lap and wonder when Mable will get out of here, when we can stop spending so much time at the hospital. "It's so weird you should say that before . . . because I see myself as someone who is always looking deeper, always trying to uncover the hidden meanings in conversations." I'm not so much hurt as I am surprised; Mable probably is right, but seeing myself through someone's else's eyes is so revealing.

Mable nods, her eyes wide. "Oh, I agree with you there, Love. I meant more that your expectations are like you assume everything will work out, that the right college will appear in front of you, or the boy you're meant to be with will suddenly proclaim his desire, or your songs will magically find their way into some famous person's mouth."

Her words settle on me like sparrows, clustering and pecking, until I say, "Yeah. That's about it. It's like I'm half counting on the path just appearing in front of me. But at the same time, if it did, would I take it? If life were this treasure hunt, would I follow it?" The camera keeps going, pointed at Mable who breathes through her nose audibly. "And the thing is, once you know something about yourself, how do you get past it? Like how do I take over the figurative reins and experience some adventure?"

Mable mimes horseback riding, then hands me invisible reins. "Like this."

Later, we're outside at the hospital's small patio café. Mable is drinking a high-calorie protein drink and I'm nursing some ice water. "I have to get my caffeine consumption under control before this summer. Can you imagine me on full-buzz at Slave to the Grind Two?" I ask.

Mable smiles and sticks out her tongue. "You're right, by the way; you do have to rename that place. Maybe you can do a promotion or something in June?"

"Yeah—that sounds good. I'll talk to Arabella about it. And you, of course."

"And Ula and Doug," Mable says. "They need to be kept in the loop about those kinds of decisions. They're part-owners now."

I don't deal with the mention of the coffee twins or ask about the business dealings. Instead I venture, "Did my dad mention anything to you about canceling my plans for the summer? Like that I wasn't going to be able to help you with the café?"

"No, why?" Mable sips her drink and pouts. "This stuff is so thick it's like drinking vanilla pudding."

"It sounds good."

"I'd offer you a sip, but you know . . ." She points to her mask. We call her Super Germ Fighter, since the mask takes over her mouth and nose, protecting her from all the viruses floating around outside.

"Your dad hasn't mentioned anything like that to me . . . but then again, he's been otherwise distracted lately. Which is a good thing. I hear you and Louisa are getting to be friends?"

I shrug. "I guess so—we've been running together. I think it helps Dad get over the three of us sitting around the breakfast table in that silence that means we all know she spent the night." I finish my water and crunch the ice cubes, giving myself a cold headache. "But she's fine . . . better than fine. She makes him happy."

"Good," Mable says and looks away. Even though it's very warm outside, Mable wears a light blue cardigan from which she pulls a worn manila envelope the size of a piece of toast. "I thought you'd like to see these," she says. "Now, don't go crazy . . . and your father doesn't know I'm showing them to you. He and I have started to disagree on some things and I don't want to go behind his back, so I will tell him that you've looked at this, but I wanted to make sure that . . ."

"Do I need a top secret decoder for this information?" I ask and take the envelope from her. "I'm assuming this has something to do with my mother? Galadriel?"

Mable winces when she hears me say that name, bringing up all my fears and confusion. "Yes. No. Kind of."

She leans forward and gives me a pictorial lesson in history. "This is where you lived when you were first born." She points to the grainy picture in my hand—it's a triangular brick apartment building set on a corner. "This was your parents' apartment."

I touch the third-floor window with my finger, trying to get close to the details. "So this is where they brought me home after the hospital?"

Mable nods and swallows. She's obviously nervous, her voice is shaky and her hands tremble slightly, though some of her medication makes her do this anyway. "Your mom wanted to have a home birth but your dad fought her tooth and nail."

"Why? Didn't he like the au naturel approach, you know, delivering on the bed?"

"No way—he was so afraid of something happening to you. He really just wanted to make sure nothing went wrong."

"That's Dad, always planning for disaster."

Mable changes her tone. "There's really nothing wrong with being prepared. David—your dad—is just cautious, that's all."

"I know," I say and look at the next picture. "Is that you?"

Mable chuckles. "Nice, huh? It was the eighties—not a great decade for hair."

We go through, looking at dated pictures of my dad, Mable, infant me (with strawberry blond hair and a toothless grin), Dad sitting on the hood of a rusting car. When we finish, I realize I'm kind of let down. "Aren't there any of Galadriel?" I ask.

Mable puts the pictures away. "Of course there are—but not right now. Another time." She pockets the past and with a look tells me it's time for me to do the same. "Now, show me that list of names and contributions for the Avon Walk for Breast Cancer."

"We're still waiting on one name—some big thing that Chris was working on," I say, but I show her the list of what we have so far.

"This is incredible," she says and smiles wide. Her eyes crinkle at the edges and then she looks at her watch. It's so big on her now that she wears it like a bracelet. "You should probably get going."

"Why, you have a big date?" I ask.

Mable swallows and shakes her head but says, "Not a date, not exactly."

I raise my eyebrows at her, and pinch my lips together. "Do tell."

When I see her ex-boyfriend, twice ex-fiancé, Miles, at the door, he waves in a sort of defeated way and I take my cue to leave.

Chapter 7

Chris has the legs of his pants rolled up and I'm in knee-high Wellington boots. We slosh through the mud and puddles on campus, enjoying the warm downpour and intentionally soaking each other. I was pretty drenched already, having gone running in the rain with Louisa while my dad wrote verbiage for some handbook that will be mailed to parents this summer.

"She's cool," I say to Chris who's been curious if Louisa is marriage material for my dad or just another datable. "I think this'll last."

"You're lucky you like her—it sounds good." Then Chris pokes me in the belly and we crack up. "I'm so psyched!"

"I know! You're incredible. I can't believe you got her to do it!"

We're celebrating Chris's big pull for the largest donation for our walk. We have most faculty signed up, tons of students, random people we've stopped on the street, Arabella, Chili Pomroy, and her parents, and—now—an enormous donation from Lindsay Parrish.

"She fell like a stack of tinned vegetables," Chris says and stomps in a puddle, coating my shirt with muddy drool.

"Is that even an expression?" I ask.

"No. I don't think it is—but who cares. All I had to do was go through her mother. Señora Parrish controls everyone, including her bitchy daughter, and when I phoned her . . ."

"With your charming English accent . . ."

"Exactly. And I told her that EVERYONE had donated—of course Madame had to be the biggest name on the list, and I promised her that if she made Lindsay donate from her own grossly cushy trust fund, that we'd list the Parrish name at the top of our thank-yous."

"Which of course we will because that's an easy thing to do."

"We rock," Chris says and gives me a damp hug from the side.

"And who else rocks?" I ask, nudging Chris for a boyfriend update and checking his expression from the side. Water runs from his hair to his ears, cascading down his nose in a steady stream. "My, it's raining."

Chris holds up his palms as if checking for drizzle. Thunder cracks over us. "Really? I hadn't noticed." Chris opens his mouth to drink the rain and, his face still skyward, says, "Well, you know how I feel about Haverford, right?"

"Yes, I'm aware of your predicament. Straight? Gay? It's anyone's guess. When are you going to act or move on?"

"You notice he's all but vanished in the past couple of weeks?" Chris asks and I give an affirmative thumbs up. "Why do you think that is?"

"I don't know. Did you scare him off or something? I mean, not everyone's going to be out in high school, you know?"

"Totally—it's like he knew but he didn't want to know; therefore he chose not to know. Or maybe he's not and doesn't want to be gay by association. He does live and act very straight."

This makes me think of Mable's critique of me, how I choose not to know certain things, too. "Maybe he wasn't ready . . ."

"Whose side are you on?" Chris asks. We sit on the Science Center wall, underneath where they showed *Grease,* and look at the wet fields.

"The gay side," I say and shake my head. "So then what happened?"

"Haverford's a waste of my time. I don't want to be anyone's turning point in their sexual identity—at least not now. It's too much pressure. So Haverford's back with the lacrosse crew, ignoring his impulses and taking out his frustration on the field."

"And what about you?" I ask.

"Poor me," Chris says and looks so sad for a second I think he'll cry. But then he instantly reverses emotions and does a smile-nod combo. "I have a boyfriend!"

"That was fast—way to get over one guy and under another," I say but Chris shakes his head.

"Not yet."

"Who's the lucky lad?" I ask. Chris shrugs. "Come on—tell me." Chris locks his mouth with a pretend key and chucks the nonexistent key onto the wet grass. I jump down from the wall, pretend to search for the thing and, once I find it, pull Chris down onto the grass with me and unlock his mimed-closed mouth.

"Okay, okay, it's Alistair the American!" Chris says as we roll around fake-fighting in the mud. "There is and I quote from the email he sent me announcing his intentions to start—or continue—a long-distance relationship, 'an ardency to his feelings that he can't ignore.' You can read the letter next time you come to my room."

"I don't mean to interrupt your mud-wrestling," Lindsay Parrish says from above us, her hands on her hips, her clothing immaculate despite the heavy rains and earth-caked sidewalks. "It does look like you have a future in the world of professional bar entertainment."

"Nice to see you, too, Lindsay," I say. "And if I haven't said congratulations on your position as Co–Head Monitor, please accept my heartfelt good wishes now." And please accept my lips on your buttocks.

I say this all from my place in the mud, so she thinks I'm groveling, but it's mainly because I just don't care. What kind of hell can she further inflict on me, really? She can't touch my grades. I'm not a Hadley student right now, and since I'll be a senior and I'm a day student, she can't govern my every move in the dorms like she does with her minions.

"Thanks for that, Love," Lindsay says in her ultrafake voice. "Chris, here's your check. I support your cause and hope the walk goes well."

"Thanks," Chris says and I nod, further caking my head in mud. I'll be gorgeous after I shower, right? Isn't mud supposed to be some natural cleanser with healing blah blah blah? Or maybe that's sand to exfoliate. Or only Icelandic mud. Oh well.

"However, in the future, if you could go through ME rather than my mother, I would be most appreciative." Lindsay lets her anger show through, her words seething.

"Of course," Chris and I say in unison.

Chris tells me again how he called Mrs. Parrish and convinced her how important a donation would be, what a statement it would be if Lindsay were to contribute the money from her own monthly stipend that comes from her trust fund.

I figure it's no big deal—when would I need to go to her mother again? For an urgent appointment at an elite spa in Manhattan maybe. Or the next time I need a Hamptons rental—i.e., never. And there's no reason why Lindsay would attempt to go through my dad to get to me. Lindsay humphs off, bearing her fancy umbrella as a shield against rain, its point seeming like a weapon.

"Great idea," I say to Chris when Lindsay's sloshed off to drier pastures.

"Yeah." Chris sits up in the mud, his arms around his knees. "Let's just hope it doesn't come with too much revenge."

"Hey, Asher, it's me—um, Love, just checking in . . . saying hi. I wasn't going to leave a message but then I figured I may as well—I mean I've already been connected by an international

operator—if they still use those for connecting purposes. I
don't know; I'm not a phone worker but . . . so . . . just . . . I
hope you're well. I got your email. It was—brief. Not just
brief, but nice, too. Oh well. Anyway, just give me a call when
you get a second. I was looking at airfares and it seems like
there are some good ones . . . Bye!"

Not one of my better messages. I really expected him to
pick up—I mean where would he be at eight in the morning
on a Sunday except asleep in his own bed? But he wasn't there,
and I'm not about to chase him down on the gallery line because then I'll just seem pathetic and lame. Plus, it's late here,
three in the morning, and I need to get some rest. I spent the
earlier part of the evening finishing my last history paper for
the last of my drama credit in London; with my persuasive
skills I managed to get them to give me partial credit if I wrote
an essay that detailed the history of theater and its political and
cultural reflections in modern-day society.

Now all that's left is a few more taping sessions and that
damn project for PMT. I don't know what else I can throw together for her—I have no novel to write, no poems to spew,
no songs unsung (okay, I have lots of songs unsung but I'd like
to keep them that way—at least for now).

I check my email one last time before going to bed, just to
make sure Asher didn't send another note—the one I received
yesterday was all of one line:

> Love—am planning a visit at the end of June—does that
> work for you?—Asher

He didn't even say he missed me. And though I hate to be a whiny girlfriend, I'm kind of annoyed. What's the point of having a long-distance relationship if you can't at least have deep longing and passionate correspondence. But maybe I'm just wrapped up in the Jane Austen fantasy of letters sealed with melted wax, bundles of love notes bound with silk ribbons. Nowhere in that historic fantasy are there one-line emails that eschew grammar and capitalization.

But before I despair, I have something in my mailbox that's new. I don't immediately recognize the name M. Eisenstein, but it's the subject "Voice Work" that doesn't sound like traditional spam of the penis enlargement/work-from-home variety, so I open it.

> **Hello Love Bukowski!**
> **Sorry to hear you had to head back to the States . . .**

It dawns on me that I am reading a personalized email from THE Martin Gregory Eisenstein, the Indie film producer. Either he must have been very bored to email me or I'm very lucky—or both.

> **As you probably guessed, we've finished the film for which we needed dubbing—so no need to bother on that front.**

And thus my shot at stardom and hearing my voice in the coolest new release are gone . . .

However, I'm heading to LA for the summer and might
have something for you there. Any chance you'll be out
that way? My wife, Teeny, and I will be having our annual
summer fete in Malibu. Feel free to come along to that
or call my assistant and tell her I told you to set up a
meeting (code word is Mercury so she knows you're
not bullshitting—it's also the password for the party).
If you do find your way out to the sunshine, please do
look me up.
Yours,
Martin

He includes his email and phone number and address as
though I even deserve to have it; I am now one step away from
all the famous numbers in Hollywood and worldwide. How
bizarre.

And do I plan to be in the California area this summer?
Why yes, yes I do. I don't know how or when, but there's no
way I'm going to miss another opportunity. Mercury. I com-
mit the code word to memory and go to sleep.

Dad is manic. He runs from one side of the room to the other,
getting everything ready.

"Dad, you're freaking me out," I say.

"We have to be prepared—it's a long way and a big day . . ."

"Hey—you rhymed!"

"Not funny." Dad looks around in case he forgot something—his sense of humor? "Did you bring the energy bars?"

"I think I have them," Louisa says and pats her bag. "They're really good, Love—made with soy nut butter and wheat crispies . . ."

I nod. "They sound great, really. I'm sure they'll be like homemade Clif Bars and everything. But I think we should go."

Chris saves the day by announcing the time and suggesting traffic and parking problems, so Dad finally takes a breath, checks for his wallet, water bottle, and then grabs an extra blanket.

"I think I'm all set," Dad says.

"Great," I say and head out the door with Louisa.

Normally, my father wouldn't be a mess—he's a calm planner. A fastidious planner, but a calm one. What's thrown him off his game (oh, sporting analogy) is that Mable was just a few days ago given the clearance to join me and Chris for the Avon Walk. The Avon Walk is the length of a marathon or more over two days. You can walk for the whole thing or just part but Chris and I are prepared to go the full distance, meaning 26.2 miles in one day and 13.1 the next. Can you say blisters? Can you say dire need of foot rub? Can you say glad to do it?

We're allowed to push Mable for exactly one mile, at which point my dad will bring her back to Mass General Hospital where she will be checked out by a team of doctors and put back to bed. She was spending a lot of time out of bed last week but got tired again this week, so her oncologist switched one of her medications around to see if it helps her feel better.

Still, her spirits are up and she's psyched to walk with us (walk=ride). So Dad's nervousness is mainly connected to Mable and his feelings of responsibility and probably sibling guilt about being well while she's sick (something I've felt, too, sometimes).

But there's something else—as though he's preparing to tell me something but can't quite bring himself to do it. Arabella and I made a list while instant messaging yesterday and the clear-cut winning guess is that Dad is about to announce his engagement to Louisa but is scared of what my reaction will be.

"This is crazy!" Mable yells from her wheelchair. The crowds are a mass of pink ribbon–sporting walkers of all ages and shapes. Husbands who have lost their wives, kids with their moms, friends linking arms with friends, grandmas, and even a couple of dogs wearing pink bandanas walk along with us. I push Mable and wave to random people.

"I feel famous!" Chris says.

"I know—it's like being on the red carpet but with this awesome group of people who are all doing the same thing for the same reasons!" We're so into it that Chris doesn't even question my lack of red-carpet experience. Instead, we just march and sip water and sing when other people sing and don't cry—because even though it's a walk born out of loss, it doesn't feel that way right now.

"Thanks for this, guys," Mable says and swivels her head so she can smile at us. She pats my hand while I grip the wheelchair's handle and we keep moving forward, our own unique story, but part of the larger crowd.

Song of the moment: "Cuts like a Knife" by Bryan Adams. It's on my *Cutlery and More* CD mix for Jacob. Sure, mixes are just like love letters for the modern age but they can also be a token of friendship, right? Plain and simple—not so overinterpreted? Let's hope so, because it's in this vein that I am collecting songs. Jacob, who still has his old DrakeFan email address, wrote and asked what I've been listening to lately. He's into a bunch of French songs from the sixties that I don't understand but try to sing along phonetically to and make Chris laugh. Jacob tried to come up with a random theme for a music share and decided I had to make a "cutlery" mix (he had just been in the dining hall at the time) and he had to put together a mix of songs with only one word as their titles. So far I have "The Lovin' Spoonful," the Brooks Williams tune "Knife Edge," and the Bryan Adams song—I'm hoping Jacob won't start picking apart the words, wondering if I'm sending a message like *I took it all for granted, how was I to know what you'd be letting go . . . ,* and so on. I'm making a mix and talking to Arabella, two of my favorite things.

"I guess we could be friends," I say to Arabella. "Even though Jacob's beautiful and being purely platonic would be a slight challenge. I mean, not now because of Asher of course, but I mean in general—you know that sexual tension thing that can ruin everything."

"Or heighten it!" Arabella says.

"Whatever, it doesn't matter now. The school year's almost

finished and once I'm on the Vineyard I'm sure I won't be thinking about Jacob."

"No, you'll be too busy hooking up with that boat boy," Arabella suggests, and I know her well enough to know she's got her eyebrows raised.

"Put those eyebrows down, Piece. I will be doing nothing of the sort. First, in case you've forgotten, I have a boyfriend." That said boyfriend being her brother is apparently of no consequence.

"Who's not there," she interjects.

I ignore her and say, "Second, Boat Boy, who has a real name by the way—Charlie—Charlie Something . . . stood me up and no one stands me up. Oh my God, how *Dirty Dancing* was that? Anyway, Charlie has nothing going for him."

"Bollocks. He's gorgeous, witty, and had that earthy man of the sea appeal."

"Earthy and of the sea? Have you been drinking?" I ask.

"A little," she says. "Oh, and I almost forgot. What about the lovely Henry? Now, he's a tuna sandwich."

"Huh?"

"I was going to say he's a lovely piece of cake, but then I remembered that you don't really like cake, so I picked something you do like, and it was very quick thinking. Sorry."

"Great, now I'll forever think of him as a tall, blazer-wearing tuna salad sandwich."

"Hang on a sec," Arabella says. I can hear her chatting away on her cell phone while I wait on the landline. "Sorry. That was Toby."

"Really?" I ask. "I didn't know you two were on speaking terms."

After they broke up, Arabella swore off boys, figuring she'd go on a boy-bender this summer and have her fill of Americana. Tobias vacationed in Nevis and slept with Lila Lawrence, my formerly of Hadley friend who now goes to Brown. I don't want to bring her name up though, just in case it causes Arabella to unleash unfriendly remarks. Plus, the last time Tobias's name came up, I believe her words regarding him were in the realm of *screw him if he thinks I'm ever speaking to him again.* And yet . . .

"Oh, well, I have good news," Arabella says, and has her rushed excited voice on. "It turns out the whole business in Nevis was just a misunderstanding! Nothing happened. Lila Lawrence was just wasted or something and when I walked in on them it was—he was just trying to help her. So it's really good news on this front."

"But . . . ," I start to say and then stop. Should I tell her about what I know? That I know for a fact that Toby did cheat on her in Nevis? That I have a saved IM from Lila Lawrence stating as much? Or is that getting in the way of things? "How can you be sure?"

Arabella clicks at me, annoyed. "When you've known someone as long as I have, the way I've been intimate with Toby, you can just tell. Besides, why would he bother lying?"

"Um, to get you back? Obviously. I mean, he knows he screwed up; he's just desperate to reclaim you as his."

"Reclaim me? I'm not his luggage."

I remember the way Tobias always had his hand on Arabella's

butt while checking out whoever passed by, the way he spoke about her in the third person, like "Oh, she'll do the dishes for you . . . ," and I want to say that I disagree, she could be his baggage. But I don't. I try another approach. "Look, everyone likes to think they can trust, but the truth of it is that once the lie is out there, once it's uttered, you have to find out more."

"I've worked all this through, Love. It doesn't matter what happened on Nevis—well, it matters a bit I guess—what matters is that Toby still loves me."

"No, what matters is do you still love him?"

Arabella uses a sigh as her response and then switches gears. "So, how was the walk?"

"Great, really good. We got so many donations and Mable was so so happy to be outside with people and sort of back to life."

"How do you think she's doing?"

I lie down on my floor, surrounded by CDs and papers and editing notes—I have tons of footage of Mable and someday soon I'll have to kiss up to the AV crew and get some help trimming it down. "Oh, I don't know. One day she's okay and the next she has a fever and is fighting some infection." I curl up into a ball and say the next words quietly. "She's fought so hard, you know? But I . . . oh, I can't even say this . . ."

"Try . . . You need to talk to someone," Arabella says.

"I don't know—somewhere, some part of me thinks she's just too tired now. Or too sick. I overheard my dad talking about hospice—and that's for people whose lives are ending, so I don't know if that's like a worst-case scenario or what."

"Lots of people survive breast cancer, Love. Think of the crowd you walked with, how many survivors there are!"

"You're right. You're right. But still, there were a lot of people there who'd lost people, too."

Arabella gives me a minute to recover and then says, "Hey, listen . . . speaking of lost people. I've been thinking about this summer, and the Vineyard and—"

"Don't tell me you're bailing out."

"No—God, no. I just wanted to ask you again—I was talking with Mum about it, you know how Monti can get going on an idea . . . and well, have you ever come right out and asked Mable if she's—"

"What?"

"If Mable is your *mother*."

I get shivers just like I had when Fizzy and Keena suggested the same thing on one of our Pizza Express evenings in London. "Don't you think that's just a bit much? Like she and my dad were married—gross. You know what? I'm done with this train of thought."

"Fine—the train has left the station. But consider this as the caboose: You once told me Mable's middle initial is *G*, right?" I nod even though Arabella can't see me. "So, your mother is Galadriel—maybe that's what the *G* stands for!"

"Enough—good-bye, Bels—and say hi to Toby for me, I think."

"I will, I think," Arabella says, and we hang up and go back to our different time zones.

Chapter 8

"You're going to be famous is what you're basically saying," Chris says.

"No, she's saying she could be if she appears at the right moment," Chili Pomroy corrects.

"You're both just not even listening to the reality of the situation," I protest. I'm still in my running gear after a morning jog with Louisa and feel like a fit but fugly stepsister around all the springy girls in their sundresses and skirts, their Nantucket red shorts worn a size too big so they rest on the hips. Chris, Chili, and I are sitting on the floor of the Art Dome, waiting for the Spring Sing to start. It's a semisweet, semilame tradition Hadley has of getting everyone together to "be as one voice." Too bad that voice is most often off tune and a full beat behind. But I digress. "The point is, it's just a casual offer that he made."

"I'm sorry," Chris says and checks his hair just in case the Hadley paparazzi show up to snap a candid of him, "but if Martin Bloody Eisenstein asks you to set up a meeting, you're in. If he asks you to go to his annual Malibu gala, you get there."

I smile and bite my lower lip. "Maybe—God that'd be so

amazing. But now I have to find a way to get to LA. It's not exactly a quick ferry ride from the Vineyard."

Our leg room is squeezed out by hoards of students, so Chili, Chris, and I are forced to scoot way up front near the raised platform stage, so we look like groupies. I mock holding a lighter up and Chili holds her cell phone up so it radiates. The Dean of Social Affairs, Lillian Frondworth, appears on stage. She is spoken of often, though rarely seen in person, inspiring students to question her existence.

"Hey, she's here!" Chris says, impressed with Lillian and her sense of late-seventies, Harvard-preppy style.

"Let's start with 'He's Got the Whole World in His Hands,' " she says animatedly and claps her hands.

"It's moments like this when you realize why certain campus events are mandatory. Can you imagine those guys coming out of choice?" Chili points to the lacrosse set, jock-preps who clap halfheartedly, her brother Haverford included. Next to Haverford is Walter Bistin who checks out a girl's cleavage by pretending he needs to fix his shoe, while Maggie Puddingtop (an unfortunate name for anyone, let alone someone bestowed with her breasts) tries to heft her boobs into their bra-harness without her long-standing crush, Alexander McGourty, seeing. I scan the faces for friends, people I haven't seen since coming back, and am relieved to find Jacob sitting, not with a female but with a couple of his dorm mates. Dorms tend to cluster together at events like this, sort of like bunks at camp.

After a parade of school songs (not "Green Though It Yet May Be," our school hymn that's only for graduation and certain assemblies and chapel services, another unwritten but known rule), Lillian Frondworth adjusts her silk scarf, restoring its jaunty position off to the side, and announces, "We have a special treat!"

"We get to go?" Chris asks wearily. "I don't know how much more forced cheer I can stand."

"At least it's air-conditioned in here," I say.

"Your tuition dollars at work," Chili says.

"She doesn't pay tuition," Chris says.

"Shut up, both of you," I say and turn my attention to the stage, which is a mere foot away.

"I'd like to introduce a couple of student musicians," Mrs. Frondworth says and we all watch as a freshman and her friends take the stage and sing a four-part harmony of "Someone to Lean On."

"So very frosh," Chris whispers.

"Shh," I say. "It's sweet—it takes guts to get up there."

"Love's right," Chili says, "even though they suck."

The next student is Claire Reading who plays the piano and sings in muffled Amos-fashion, with highs, lows, and indistinguishable lyrics. Mrs. Frondworth is clearly unable to tell what the hell Claire is saying but claps enthusiastically and says, "Well done, Claire!"

Just when I think we're done and ready to make a mass exodus toward the dining hall, I look up on the stage and see Jacob there, tuning a guitar.

"I didn't know he played guitar." Chris looks at me, his mouth its own question mark.

"Me, neither," I say but can't break my gaze from Jacob. "I thought he was just a piano player."

Chili uses a breathy voice. "Maybe there's a lot you don't know about Mr. Coleman."

I don't answer her; I just listen to him play. The chords start, a little familiar, then as he gets going, I recognize the song completely. *Like a fool I went and stayed too long, now I'm wondering if your love's still strong . . .*

"Hey, this is 'Signed, Sealed, Delivered,' " Chris says.

I nod. It's the Stevie Wonder song Jacob put on my mix sophomore year before we were even a couple. It's the one that always makes me think of him, even when I was in England and Asher played it for me. Does Jacob remember putting this song on my disk? Or was that just coincidence? His acoustic version is incredible—slow in the right parts, alive and insistent in others—the crowd loves it and when he's done, everyone claps hard, loving the cool, new, Euro-fied Jacob. And he—JC—as he's affectionately known now, drinks it in. Gone is the shy funny person from sophomore year and from my recent run-in at the college counseling office—his public persona is decidedly hip. But maybe it's just a stage thing.

"You look weird, Love," Chris says. "You look the way I must have when I got a letter from Alistair saying he missed me. Like I'd seen a ghost."

"That was kind of, um, our song he just played . . . ," I say super-spacey and suddenly tired.

"Oh dear," Chris says. We stop outside the dining hall and

he waits for me to emerge from my Jacob-induced haze. "Maybe it was a message? Or maybe it meant nothing?"

"You know what, it doesn't matter," I say immediately back in the moment. "I have a life—I have a boyfriend, I have friends, and I have a good shot at a fun summer and . . ." I drift off. "I'm not up for public displays of emotion—I'm going to go see Mable."

Chris nods. "Tell her the final amount we raised."

"I will. Bye, you guys." I walk to my car as Chris and Chili walk inside.

I check voice messages, hoping there'll be one from Asher, but yet again I am left with no vocal rendering of his feelings, not even a trace. When I spoke to Arabella to get her pledge for the Avon Walk, I came right out and asked her what the hell Asher's deal was. Her clear response was, "Love, I told you from the outset that I was not going to be put in the middle of your relationship with my brother. I made that completely clear to you—and to him—so please don't start now. If you guys wind up getting married and having twelve kids, great. If you shag, fine. If you break up, I'll comfort you. But I don't want to play messenger nor do I want the responsibility of picking apart Asher's actions." Thus, she's not shedding any light on the current situation. And I don't blame her, not really—a little, because she might know something I don't—but I just wish Asher would tell me his thoughts.

I have one phone message, though, from Clementine Highstreet, my famous London friend, saying she only just got my note asking for a donation for the Avon Walk. She's "thrilled to make a contribution," she says and hopes we'll "have the good fortune" to see each other again. Her voice makes me think of my time with her and of her song, "Like the London Rain," which I know Mable would love to hear. I search my side door and glove compartment but don't find a disk with that song on it, so I head to my room to locate it.

When I enter my room, I am hit on the head—literally— by *The Oliver P. Barley Guide to Colleges*. First I swear and then I crouch to pick it up. I play one of those games that make no sense but that you do to feel like you have control over your world. Whatever page the book landed on is where I should go to college. I slide my finger underneath like a bookmark and turn it over to see where my fate will lead me—page ninety-eight, the beginning of "Schools of the North East." Um, sure, but could you maybe be a little more specific? After all my meetings with the college counseling office to talk about planning my visits and writing my essays, I am at turns wracked with nerves and then way too mellow about where I'll go. I just keep waiting for a sign. But aren't signs just another way of trying to get out of making the decisions on your own?

I change out of my running clothes and into khaki shorts and my dad's old Harvard T-shirt. It makes me think of the Vineyard and wearing it there when I first met Charlie out at sea (after all he is so earthy and such a man of the ocean, as Arabella so aptly said). It's funny how clothing can hold so many memories. Sometimes I look at all my sweaters or shirts and wonder about all the different days I've worn them, the regular afternoons when I did homework, days when I went to class, ate, slept and then the days that stick out for some reason or other: fought with Dad about London (blue V-neck T-shirt), played soccer by myself for hours, wishing someone would join me (jeans with green paint stain on the thigh), got very close to sleeping with Asher (white bra with the clasp that sticks out a little and scratches my back, but I can't get rid of it because of aforementioned memory), sang Barry Manilow and laughed and then cried with Mable (ugly purple shirt she told me looked like a prune had vomited on me).

In light of this, I find a new T-shirt, a soft pink one that makes me feel free and summery, and toss the Harvard one back in my drawer. I pull the Gap tags off and check out the shirt in the mirror—yep, it's pink, it's clean, it's fine. Then the phone rings.

"I need you," says Mable into the phone and my heart leaps to my mouth.

"I'll be right there," I say, find a copy of "Like the London Rain," and slide it into my bag.

"Let me finish," she says. "I need you to do me a favor."

I breathe a sigh of relief—sort of. "What—anything."

"I know it's out of the way—and I know the lines are long right now, but if I get one of the nurses to call in an order, will you go to Bartley's Burgers and pick me up some lunch?"

Suddenly, nothing in the world sounds better than getting take-out from the best burger place in Boston, and sitting eating fries and a frappé with Mable. "Of course," I say. "But I'm getting sweet potato fries, so you get regular."

"That way we can each have some of both."

It's what we've always done with food—like when you can't decide and want two things, we always want the same two things, so we swap. As I think this, I look at myself in the mirror. My mouth, my green eyes, the cheekbones that appear to be more prominent than they were when I was younger. The freckles on my jaw and nose—just like Mable's. Maybe she could be my mother. Or maybe I'm just in dire need of food.

I've done the drive from Hadley to Harvard Square enough times that I have a little back route I like to take, driving in third gear on Brattle Street, past the huge old homes and weaving into the cluttered academic area near the shops. Unable to find a parking meter, I snag a resident parking spot and hope I don't get a ticket. Then I figure if I do it's money well spent—if Mable craves a Bartley's meal, then she should have it.

The streets are less crowded now, the college students have dispersed for summer break, and the ones who remain don't walk in herds with books and bags; they sit with iced coffees outside, lolling in the warm day, watching old guys play chess and buskers sing. I stand and watch a woman play guitar. She sings a song she presumably wrote and has a couple of her own CDs available for purchase. Would I ever stand on a street corner and sing? It's hard to imagine I would unless it were on a dare. Maybe this means I just don't want to sing as badly as I once thought I did. In fact, I really haven't done all that much singing, save for my Carly concert at the music buildings.

With a sinking feeling, I walk past the stores and students toward Mr. Bartley's and consider that maybe I'll just be one of those adults who sings loudly in the car but leads an otherwise regular life, job, house, kids, whatever. Or maybe I would stumble into some other cool field—I still love music and I still like singing. It just isn't a driving force for me anymore. I try to think if this is in reaction to Mable or just getting older or what, but it's hard to differentiate between life events on the outside and what's happening in my head. My best guess is that I was always more interested in the lyrics than the music—and if art is a way of expressing yourself, maybe my true art is in the words, not the song. Then again, give me a chance to sing or put my voice into a Martin Eisenstein movie and I'd be thrilled.

Even though Mable's nurse called in the order, I feel compelled to go over the specifics of it, to make sure her food will be perfect. "One order of regular fries, please, and one sweet potato. A Kraft burger with sautéed onions and a Messy Special." I look at the menu boards—several oversized chalkboards that hang from the ceiling—to make sure I haven't forgotten anything. "Oh, and vanilla frappé—extra thick." I like frappés regular, more on the milkshake side but Mable prefers hers to be nearly impossible to suck through a straw. I pay and wait at one of the small tables off to the side while my order cooks.

Looking around, I can see ghost images of myself—when I first came here with Mable, when I came here with Lila Lawrence on a double date with my first Hadley crush,

Robinson Hall, and his friend, Channing. When I brought Arabella here and she ate three orders of sweet potato fries in one sitting, then sat nursing an oil-hangover on one of the benches in Harvard Yard afterward and we'd named the various squirrels we'd seen.

I try to picture Asher here, imagine him at one of the communal tables, sharing relish and spicy mustard, but I can't. In fact, when I try to picture him visiting, I have a clear vision of parading him around campus, of being psyched to be with him, but I can't get past the feeling that he exists only in England. Or Paris. Somewhere European. Someplace with castles. Should I break up with him? The thought is revolting but also makes sense. How could I have been so close to sleeping with him and now haven't heard from him after leaving five messages?

Then, my posterior seems to vibrate and I reach for my phone. The caller's ID is listed as "withheld," which usually means Mable's calling from her room phone.

"I got the goods," I say as my hello.

"Which goods might those be?" Asher asks.

"Oh, hi!!!" I say so enthusiastically the exclamation points are hanging in the air for all to witness. Hearing his voice makes all my prior thoughts of breaking up or never kissing him again seem remote and like a big mistake.

"Sorry sorry—a million times sorry about not ringing you back sooner. My excuse is that I was in Scotland with very poor cell phone reception and no landline."

"Why? Were you at a castle or something?" I say, joking with myself about my earlier vision.

"Yes, I was—how did you know?" Asher asks but doesn't wait for me to respond before he goes on. "It started off with just me and Valentine. She's mad as I've mentioned before but in this very mobilizing way."

Cue the return of my doubts. "Insane like a highway?"

"What? Oh, right. Anyway, we just suddenly got this idea to try to get these fringe artists together to form a sort of collective and bring a traveling show—imagine a massive mural that contains pieces that work separately but then also forms a whole entity . . ."

I swear I'm listening to him, I'm hearing what he's saying, and I like how excited he is about his work. But I can't stop hearing the first part . . . It started off with just me and Valentine. In a bed? On a beach? In a pub? Where were the two of them as they suddenly got inspired with artistic groove and created their little minstrel show? "It sounds really interesting," I say.

"But what about Scotland?" he asks.

Clearly, I missed something. "Scotland?"

"Yes, it's a small country that's gray and windy and filled with Scottish people," Asher says. "I asked if you had interest in coming to the festival with me. The Edinburgh Art Festival is world famous, you know. It's in August . . ."

"Wow—August—I'd love to go to Scotland. With you. But would you still come here?" It sounds petty but I really wanted him to see my life—I know where he lives, who his friends are, but he's never met my dad nor met Mable. Plus, I like the idea of making out with him in front of Lindsay Parrish, even though that's about as superficial and petty as I can admit to being. And . . . what about that infamous next step? I was fairly ready in London, but maybe I'd be very ready here on home turf. Or maybe having Asher here with me would make me less sure. It's all confusing and muddled, which probably means it's not an immediate course of action. But I can think about it, dissect it, and wonder. Plus, he hasn't even said he'd visit.

"Of course I'm still visiting—I said I would—and I'm always good on my word," Asher says. "And I saw Arabella yesterday. She's really looking forward to your summer. She showed me photos of your cottage."

"Yeah, we're actually not living there, though. I thought we were but . . ." My voice sinks a little as I explain. "It turns out it's rented for part of the summer, so Mable figured it was easier just to sublet the space above the café. So we'll be up there. Which is pretty convenient."

The counter guy yells my order number and rings a bell, and I make may way over to pick up the delicious, artery-clogging food. "Well, just tell me when and I'll pick you up at Logan," I say and hand the cashier some money.

"I'll let you know soon, all right?" Asher pauses. "Is there anything else you wanted to tell me? Something we haven't talked about? Your messages seemed pretty insistent."

I collect my change and wonder if now is the time to talk about my feelings, my insecurities—valid or not—about Valentine, how I want to know what Asher's take is on a long-distance relationship, and on and on. But as I figure out how best to start off, I collide—as in chest to chest—with Charlie.

I am this close to saying, "Boat Boy!" just out of the sheer shock of seeing him in all his rugged glory. A) Seeing him at all and B) seeing him in Harvard Square. It's totally close-minded of me but it's as though I assumed he never left the island of Martha's Vineyard, and if he did it wouldn't be to go to the mecca of all things academic. Actually, right now he isn't so much rugged as prugged, a preppy-rugged, not that I'd describe him as preppy to his face because he would rather whip himself with a whale belt than wear one, but his rough edges don't seem as rough as they did the last time I saw him. Which was, of course, in the romantic fireside glow at the cottage. Before he stood me up.

It doesn't even occur to me to come right out and ask what the hell he's doing here in Cambridge, plus I don't want to insult him—I mean, people who live on Martha's Vineyard year-round do leave the island—it's not like he's a fisherman bound to his boat forever. Even if that was my mental image of him.

But I manage not to say anything except, "Oh, crap!"

Of course I have my cell phone pressed to my ear and Charlie has ranted before about my public phonage but he doesn't say anything. In the movie version of this he would either walk away without saying anything or have some witty line, but the reality of the moment is this:

My frappé spills onto my new pink T-shirt (granted, it was in the sale bin for only three dollars, but still) and forms a sticky icy web between my front and Charlie's chest.

"I take it from your silence that you don't have anything to say," Asher says and I click into action remembering I'm on an international call.

"I'm an idiot," I say into the phone, trying to shake off the extra milkshake but succeeding only in splattering more onto Charlie who looks half-amused and half like he'll press charges.

"Love, we need to talk," Asher says, very serious.

"Do you want a towel?" Charlie asks me. He grabs a stack of waxy paper napkins and tries to wipe my shirt off and brushes against my boobs in the process, which embarrasses us both and makes me drop the rest of the frappé on the floor.

"Asher, I have to go—I made a mess here," I say.

"No," he corrects me. "I've made a mess and I'm sorry. I really am."

So there, right in the middle of Bartley's, right in the middle of crashing into Charlie and Vineyard past, in the middle of picking up a simple burger, my life gets further complicated.

"Can you stay a second?" Charlie asks. "I wanted to explain—"

"I can't . . . ," I start to say and then I shake my head and hand him the damp sticky napkins as a consolation for bolting. "See you?" I ask over my shoulder and go outside.

I walk to the car, all the while listening to Asher. My hands are glued together with leftover spillage, the burgers are seeping through the white paper bag, and the fries have left an oil stain on my khakis. The frappé has formed an adhesive bond and made my hair into sticky points. I am truly a mess.

"Can you talk for a minute?" Asher asks. He sounds far

away, distant from the happy buzz of the Square, and it's a lonely feeling, talking to him from one place here while he's off somewhere completely different, experiencing a totally separate world.

"Sure," I say and take a seat on one of the metal chairs that's bolted to the ground outside a sandwich shop. A block away, Charlie—and yes, I'm blushing as I realize I don't know his last name—is dealing with the stain on his shirt, the frappé speckles on his legs and forearms. Those forearms. Oh dear.

"I'm so glad you say that you think things are mess," Asher says.

"Oh, no I'm not *glad* glad—I was just . . ." I try to explain the milkshake debacle but before I can, Asher is giving a monologue.

"I love you, Love. I do."

"You do?" I smile. My gorgeous English boyfriend loves me. Forget Charlie's forearms.

"I do. But."

"But? There's a but after the love thing?" I can't believe he's got a but. A butt, yes, a but? No.

"When you and I met I was actually in the throws of ending something with someone."

My stomach lurches. He never thought to tell me this before? Or did he really mention it and in my gushy haze it slipped by? Do I really just overlook what I don't want to deal with? Suddenly I have no desire to even be near French fries, let alone a burger.

"But I've been sorting through the various . . ."

Ways to say I love you? Plane tickets and they're expensive? Problems but I'm sure we can fix them?

"Asher—are you saying what I think you're saying?" My feet flip-flop against the pavement even though I'm not going anywhere. And, apparently, neither is this relationship. Fifteen minutes ago I thought about breaking up with him but it feels much worse now, having him do it.

"I never planned on falling for someone—you—so soon after being in a relationship—and it's not your fault, that's not what I'm implying here."

"I didn't even know about that relationship." I say it like *relationship* is synonymous with rabies.

"Of course you didn't—we just got swept up in the magic of your being here and . . ."

"You make it sound like it wasn't real." I fight off crying because I don't want to be that girl crying while sitting outside talking on her cell phone, and I can't go to the car because then I'd have to walk and cry, and the air-conditioning is broken so I would overheat.

"Remember when we were on the houseboat, lying there, having that discussion?"

I nod and say, "Yeah." It seems like one of those memories now that I'll always be able to describe but that feels impossibly far away, like those photos Mable showed me of her and my dad before I was born.

"I want that—"

"I want that, too," I say.

"But I want it all the time—the long-distance part of this

won't work for me. It feels wrong. I walk around missing you and so I'm not really in my life here."

"So it's worth trashing it all because you can't have it every day?"

"Most of life is every day, Love." Asher sighs. Or maybe he's crying, I can't tell. "And I just don't want to feel bad all the time because I'm not calling you or haven't booked a ticket and even if I did visit it would just be a Band-Aid for the larger cut."

"The way you say it makes sense," I say and let him hear me cry. "But it feels wrong to break up."

"Then perhaps we could call it something else," Asher suggests in his calm English tone.

"Like semantics are going to make this better? What if you visited and we saw how it went, you know, took it as a trial thing?"

"I don't think that's a wise idea." Asher sighs and breathes into the phone. "If I were to see you—to be with you—I'm pretty sure I couldn't end things at all . . ."

I sit up straight—taking this as my tiny window of opportunity. "So that's the answer—let's be together in person and we'll realize breaking up isn't—"

"But it is the answer, Love. For me, anyway."

"Oh." I don't know what else to say. I don't want to be clingy and needy even though part of me feels exactly that. So I stay quiet until my tears dry, sticky on my face, and Asher coughs.

"I've got to run now, but let's catch up soon."

"Bye," I say and think about how much can change in one phone call. I started off as someone's girlfriend and now, as I press the END button on my phone, it hits me that that's just what this is for me and Asher.

I don't listen to anything on the way to Mass General because whatever song came on would just be ruined as "that song I heard right after Asher Piece and I broke up," so I drive with the windows down, the breeze its own mellow music.

At the hospital, I'm busy having an out-of-body post-end of serious relationship experience so I don't notice someone saying my name over and over. In my mind I'm hearing Asher say *Love* the way he did in London, with the emphasis on the *L* part. Now I won't hear it anymore except when we randomly cross paths, such as if Arabella gets to be a famous actress and I go see her movie premiere and he's there.

"Love? Love. Love!"

Margaret Randall, Mable's favorite nurse, taps me gently on the shoulder and I welcome myself back to the waking world. "I know you've brought food for Mable—she's been mentioning that frappé all day. We were going to ask the kitchen to send one up but Mable said not to bother if you were coming."

"Oh," I say. I try not to cry again when I explain that I've come without the frozen goods, just lukewarm smushed burgers and soggy fries. "I'll go get her one from the cafeteria."

A knock at the door makes us both look over. "No, I'll go, you visit," offers Henry Randall, Margaret's nephew and my quasi-buddy from the Vineyard.

"Hey, Henry," I say and it's only slightly as lackluster as I feel.

He comes over and hugs me—not lingering like *boy, I've missed you even though I hardly know you,* and not *I want you so badly.* It's just a reasonable hello. In fact, all of him seems reasonable. He's friendly but not effusive (see, that SAT verbal studying really did pay off) and asks thankfully not about my year at Brown (where he still thinks I go) and not about Mable but about the summer.

"I heard you went abroad," he says. "I studied in Florence for a semester."

Suddenly it dawns on me that tons of American girls have had this experience. College women or graduate students go to different countries and fall in love and it doesn't work out. Then maybe they visit that country a decade later and remember those kisses they had near some monument, but basically it's all just one long postcard or photo or—for me—journal entry.

"I did—but I'm back now, obviously, right, I mean I'm standing here . . . and getting ready to head to Edgartown for the summer. Will you be there?"

"I'm on my way down right now," Henry says and reveals his car keys as proof. "I'll be up and down a little for the next month, then down for good. My dad's got a bunch of properties that just went on the market for the summer season, so I have to go manage them."

"You're selling real estate?"

Henry grins and shuffles his feet a little, exactly like the used-car salesman I just called him. "No—not exactly. But between the rental and the properties for sale, I'm doing an internship of sorts."

"Meaning you sleep late and show up when you feel like it?" I joke.

"Pretty much, yeah. Except when my father throws a fit and decides I need a lesson in hard work."

I look toward Mable's room. "I'm really late getting here," I say and back away from Margaret and Henry. "These were supposed to be emergent." I gesture with the take-out bags.

"Well, will I see you soon?" Henry asks. I nod.

My kiss on her cheek wakes Mable up. "Delivery," I say.

"You just missed your dad," Mable says and motions for me to put the food down on the table and sit with her in bed. "I'm not so hungry anymore."

"Now I feel guilty—like I missed your window of hunger."

"Don't feel guilty—it's a useless emotion. But do explain why."

So I tell her about Bartley's and Asher's prolonged phone call and bumping into Charlie. Mable nods and listens—really listens like she always does and hears what I say, not interrupting me even for a second. I start to cry and Mable says, "I can't hold it in anymore—you're crying over spilled milkshake!"

It's lame but I crack up anyway and ask her why her room is a mess. There are piles of paper and pens and books with photos sticking out of them, balled up legal pad paper, its bright yellow visible from across the room.

"Did you have a decorating party that I missed?"

Mable shakes her head, then rests it again on the pillow. "No—I was just writing some things down, organizing."

I study her face. She studies mine. I want to ask her—are you my mother—but I can't. It sounds so crazy, so far-fetched that I'm scared it might be true.

But Mable knows I have something on my mind, so I tell her this: "I'm almost done with the film—the documentary that made me documental." She laughs. "I got one of the nice AV people to help me and now there's some voice-over and you talking, plus that footage from the Avon Walk. It's not going to win a nomination or anything, but it's pretty good."

"Just think—I finally got my chance at being a movie star."

There's a finality to her words that gets to me. "This isn't your only chance—I mean, if you wanted to be an actress you could . . ."

"Love—relax. I never wanted to be an actress. Can you imagine me on a set? I'd be busy directing the director and getting fired before anyone even said *cut*."

"I was only saying that you could still change careers if you wanted to. Aren't you always telling me that, that it's never too late to go after what you want?"

Mable shrugs and closes her eyes a little. She looks small, like a doll I had once that I hugged so much bits of her yarn hair and apple-button nose wore off. "That's my advice to you. Not for me."

"So what haven't you gone after that you really wanted?" I ask.

Mable exhales out her nose and puts her hands on her belly, smoothing the sheets. "I got what I wanted, I think." I hug her and wish I could take her home with me so we could order in Chinese and sit with our backs on either end of the couch, our feet touching. "No, wait. Scratch that. Life keeps coming at you, so you peck at it like birds do, you know bobbing your head here, clucking over here."

"This is a chicken analogy?"

Mable smiles but keeps her eyes closed. "It's totally not working, is it?"

"No way," I say.

A knock at the door. Margaret comes in and hands me a large cup. "Henry got this for you," she says and leaves.

"Feel like a frappé?" I ask Mable and she suddenly sits up to take a sip.

"Now this, this is the secret to a good life." Mable swallows and goes back for another mouthful.

"The ice cream philosophy?" I ask and watch her.

"Yeah—work with me here—it's sweet, composed of some good things like milk and sugar . . ."

"And it doesn't last, so you have to appreciate it while you have it." We lock eyes over the milkshake and don't say anything else; we just sit there, appreciating.

Chapter 9

Heaped in among the dirty laundry is the pink T-shirt from today. Even as I shove it down with the rest of the week's wash, I can't discard the memories attached to it. First there's the stain. Though it will technically come out in the wash, its impact will be permanent in my mind.

This is the shirt I was wearing when Asher dumped me. This is the shirt I was wearing when I cried in public in Harvard Square. This is the pink top I had on when I got the feeling that Mable was slipping away—for real—and came home to find my father bawling in his study, affirming my feelings.

"She's not doing well," Dad says and keeps crying. He's in his desk chair, the Hadley chair that is given to each faculty member upon hiring. It has the Hadley crest on its seat and on its back, but Dad is leaning back so you can't see this.

"I just saw her," I say.

"I know—I left right before you got there," he said. "I was hoping to meet you there so we could discuss some things."

"Like what?" I ask. It's horrible to see my dad cry. His eyes are red and puffy and he looks torn apart, really so ruined, that

I can't respond with tears. I respond with not one trace of sadness, keeping my face as calm as I can, everything else shoved inside.

"I'm not going to bother you with the medical issues . . . I just wanted you to know that at this juncture . . ."

"Juncture sounds like you're a president or being a principal," I tell him. Not in a mean way, I just want him to be honest.

"Mable is not likely to recover. The best thing we can do now is to keep her comfortable and be with her . . ." Dad's tears are quiet now. I remember reading for my big drama paper about anticipatory studies some playwrights did in order to get to know how their characters would act in a given situation. It seems like Dad is doing this now, anticipating grief before he feels it—or maybe he's feeling it now so he won't have to later.

"But there's still a chance, right? Isn't there always a chance?" I pick at the sticky stain on my pink T-shirt and wish I could throw the thing away. But I won't. It will just sit in my drawer not being worn.

Dad gets up and puts his arms around me. "I don't know, Love. I'm just not sure."

In my journal is a list of reasons Mable could be my mother—not proof so much as plausibility. Here's what I know: She used to be married to a man named David—she told me that last year when I found an old photo of her sitting near a green VW van. My dad's name is David—they could be the same guy. She and my dad could have made a pact to raise me separately but together, with her living nearby but—so as not to pollute my brain with divorce—they make her my aunt. I admit it gets less and less believable as the idea progresses, but it might be true. The only thing I can't work out though is why they wouldn't have told me by now.

I call Arabella and tell her about Mable and how grim things are here. When I get to the part about my journal list Arabella says, "Look, Love, just ask her. It sounds like time-wise you should probably get . . ."

I don't want to hear what she has to say about limited time, so I cut her off. "You're right—I'll just do it. It's not like I haven't made a fool of myself in front of her before."

"How's your dad taking it?"

"Well, there's not much 'it' to take right now, just more of this looming dread I have. But not well, in answer to your question. He's beginning to suffocate me. If I'm in the kitchen, he's in the kitchen. If I'm doing laundry, he needs to wash his shirts; if I want to flip around and see what there is to watch at eleven at night, well, he's going to sit there with me."

"He's reassuring himself you're not leaving, too," Arabella says. I can hear her playing piano in the background and wonder why it is I'm always drawn to people who can play. I can easily imagine her in the flat we shared with her feet bare and her hair loose around her shoulders, her hand plucking music from nowhere and pressing the keys until they lull me to sleep.

"I know. I get the psychology here but it doesn't make my day to day very pleasant. He's so busy crying and hugging me and asking me what I feel that I can't say anything—mainly because it's as though if I show any emotions, he's going to completely lose it."

"I know this goes without saying, but I'm so sorry, Love. And I'm sorry about Asher. If it's any consolation, he showed up here drunk and sad and saying he made a mistake."

I brighten just the tiniest bit. "It doesn't matter in the grand scheme of things."

"But it does, and you know Mable wouldn't want you to ignore the rest of your life because of her illness. So even though you're guilty and you feel ashamed for still liking boys or being hungry or feeling annoyed at your dad, you have to allow yourself to do those things, to feel those things."

"Um, do you have a degree in counseling or something you haven't told me?" I ask and put away my folded laundry, shoving the pink shirt way way to the bottom of my drawer with the things I never wear yet insist on keeping.

Arabella gives a small laugh. "No, but Dad's a playwright who firmly believes in character studies, so I read one of them and this is kind of a similar situation except that the character was a man in his twenties in Ireland during the potato famine."

"Oh, but otherwise, just like this."

"Exactly," she says.

Chris is gone all weekend to visit Alistair the American who claims the title of his First Real Boyfriend (or Ferb as we've been saying—Ferbie if we're giddy), so I spend my time making piles of stuff in my room that have no rhyme nor reason.

Stuff to give away, over here. Academic stuff I need to complete over there. Books that require returning stacked on my desk. Or, no, I'll put those downstairs. I am relegated to my room by choice just to avoid Dad and his neediness. The times Dad's at the hospital, I'm free to wander downstairs or go running. I even went to the music building for a little song therapy but couldn't motivate myself once I was there. And maybe I had hoped to bump into Jacob again but I knew he wouldn't be there—not because I'm all-knowing but because I actually got up the guts to "be friends" with him and went to his dorm for a visit. But I checked his sign-out card and sure enough he's signed out for the whole weekend to some day student's house where he's probably reveling in the near end of school and his popularity that affords him top pick of the Hadley crop (the fact that I can now count myself among the corn and wheat is just not something I want to deal with).

"Where do you want to eat tonight?" Dads asks. He's slacked off on his squash games, been spending more time at the hospital and with Louisa, and has memorized most of the take-out menus we keep in the drawer by the kitchen phone.

"Aren't you seeing Louisa?" I ask (ask=hope).

"She's closed for inventory," Dad says. "Not her personally, obviously, but her store is. She closes every year at this time. She won't emerge from the book cave until Monday, so you and I have tons of time to be together."

Again. Encore. I love him but he's smothering me. I want to be with him, but like it was, not like it is now.

"I'm actually heading out myself," I say.

Dad's mouth rumples. "For the whole weekend?"

"No—not the whole weekend. Just the night."

"Where are you heading?" He flips through menus as a way of making his question seem incidental rather than part of his need to know where I am every second of the day.

I hold my cell phone in one hand, keys in the other and make an impromptu decision. "I'm going to see Mable at the hospital and then going to Newport to spend the night at Lila Lawrence's."

"Doesn't her mother have a bit of an alcohol problem?" Dad asks like he's just inquired as to whether Lila's mother enjoys a nice round of golf.

"I think *a bit* is semi-understating it, but yes, not that that stopped you from letting me visit last summer. Anyway, her mother's in Palm Springs."

"So there's no adult present?" Dad puts the menus down and looks at me.

"Lila's over eighteen, she's an adult," I suggest. Not mentioning the fact that I'm about to spend the whole summer unattended.

"Really, Love—that doesn't count. I'm sorry, I can't let you go. Go see Mable; then come back here and we'll get chimichangas."

"I hate chimichangas."

"No, you don't—you ate them all the time," Dad insists and pushes the El Corazón menu at me.

"When I was six, maybe," I say.

"Fine—then we'll order from somewhere else. Or I could come with you and we could visit Mable together."

"You just went this morning and we were there together yesterday."

We stand looking at each other, me with my keys and cell phone at my hips as though they're in a holster and Dad with his sacred take-out selections. We're at a draw.

"Fine—go to Mass General, but don't go the back way. There's a game at Fenway and you'll be stuck in traffic."

"Okay." I nod. I feel at turns like I'm twelve years old, or a hundred, but not really my true age. Not until I get to the car, settle into the front seat, put the visor down to check and see if there's really a foreign object in my eye (eyelash, piece of grass, dust) or just that irritating feeling in my eyeball that makes me pull my eyelid down twelve times in basset hound mode to check. No foreign object in my eye, but a disk drops into my lap from its position tucked away into the visor. I open the case and read the scrawled note inside:

Love—Am away this weekend but didn't want you to think I forgot about the mix. When do I get my Cutlery one? Here's my go at one-word songs. I tried to avoid too many name songs since that felt like cheating—plus, they kind of suck (Amanda, Alison, Gloria not withstanding—even "Cecelia" is one of Paul Simon's lamer tunes, don't you think?) Someday I vow to write a name song about the dog I don't yet own and make it a good song. Anyway, the liner notes are on the disk itself.—J.

"One"—U2   "Persuasion"—Tim Finn
"Centerfold"—J. Geils Band   "Africa"—Toto
"Aurora"—Bjork   "California"—Joni Mitchell
"Songbird"—Fleetwood Mac   "Candy"—Martin Sexton
"Nobody"—Tom Waits   "Mother"—Pink Floyd
"Rain"—Madonna   "Strip"—Adam Ant
"Mess"—Ben Folds Five   "Blackbird"—The Beatles
"Trouble"—Coldplay

I'm pleased to note he didn't sign his note *JC* or with some Swiss expression that translates into "Wear your rabbit slippers and the mountains will find you smiling," or something. But it does register that he leaves out what exactly his weekend plans are. Are we friends? Kind of—I mean, enough to swap CDs, but are we hanging out on the weekends, tuned into each other's lives? Not really. It's both comforting and blah-making (blah-making=pseudodepressing when it's not an issue worthy of that giant word but still something that bugs you).

I flip the visor up, put in the disk, and drive, determined not to read too much into the songs. Sure, "Centerfold" is about seeing a girl naked and lusting after her, but so far I haven't posed nude and don't plan to—and "Persuasion" has that line, *I'll always be a man who's open to persuasion,* but that doesn't mean that's what Jacob feels. Not necessarily.

One of the reasons I haven't completed his mix is because cutlery is a difficult theme around which to build a CD. I'm also hyperaware of the mix tape/CD as holder of the hidden feelings phenomenon and I just can't cope with the pressure of finding songs that remain as neutral as I am supposed to feel. Not supposed to, as neutral as I *do* feel, a "getting to know you all over again" kind of friendship. Several degrees warmer than cold, but not quite fuzzy.

When I hear "Mother" it makes me miss the hospital exit, so I have to loop around in the ever-changing mess of Boston's roads while my mind wanders from imagining what my dad was like as a twenty-something to wondering if I will lose my nerve to ask Mable if maybe I am her daughter.

"Before I lose my nerve, I have to just ask you something," I say when I'm not even all the way inside her room. Mable is sitting upright in bed; she looks close to her normal self, though I have to admit that I've begun to forget what she looked like a year ago, before all of this, before I knew cancer terminology, before I'd ever seen her cry from pain (I had seen her cry after cutting onions and after one big breakup, but she's not a big wailer).

Mable studies me for a second. "Oh my God—is this about sex? Did you do it—are you okay? Do you need anything—or no, wait—you're going to aren't you—oh, I'm so glad you came to me first."

I watch the slow but steady drip of fluid from the bulbous bag on the IV pole as it runs its course into her veins and walk over so I can hold her hand. She likes me to give her a gentle massage by squeezing her fingers one at a time.

"Um, no." I keep my lips pressed together and sit on the bed with her, resting one of my arms on the bedrail for balance. "I am not having sex today. In fact, that memorable day or night has been pushed off into the unknown for an indeterminate amount of time, but I appreciate the reminder that I'm newly single with no prospects."

"First of all, you always have prospects. You just don't always see them or see yourself as a viable option, Miss Lady Sings the Virginity Blues. Second of all, and I know I'll sound like your mother, but there's nothing wrong with waiting."

I swallow hard at the "sound like your mother" part and skip over the sex talk. As far as I'm concerned it'll happen when I say it happens and it's unlikely to occur right now, so I can fast forward and get to the real reason for my visit.

"Mable?" I ask. Big breath in. Release. "This is crazy—I know it's . . . but I have to ask because I just need to know and I've been getting the feeling that you'll tell me the truth now but only if I find the right way to ask or not the right way, but find the courage. So . . ." Mable looks at me expectantly and my heart pounds so loudly I'm sure she can hear it even over the pulse monitor's bleep and the off and on announcements from the hallway.

"Are you my mother?" I ask. I sit perfectly still and wait to hear what she says.

Mable has her eyes cast downward toward her lap and when she lifts them, she's crying. Tears spill over her sunken cheeks, dripping off her protruding jaw and landing with a tiny plunk on the crisp white sheets. I don't know if the tears are because she is or isn't or because she's horrified that I asked or if I've opened some old wound that I shouldn't have.

In the middle of her crying Mable smiles. "That would be nice, wouldn't it?"

"So, you're not?" I ask.

Mable cries harder and shakes her head. "It's a little creepy to think about. Very Greek tragedy. But also . . ." She starts to wipe the tears on the back of her hand. I reach for the tiny paper tissues on the side table and manage to pull out nearly the entire contents. I hand her the stack. "But . . ." She grabs my arm hard. "Can't you just see us, reuniting, or wait—no— you and I would have had this relationship all along but you'd have to now reflect on what it meant that I turned out to be your mom . . ."

"You're sounding very made-for-TV movie," I say.

"Well, come on, if ever there were a MFTVM with us, it's right now!"

"Yeah." I feel disappointed. But I also feel relieved. It's one thing to grow up with no real notion of who my mother is, what happened—although I guess I know by now that she left—but it's another thing to think that on top of Mable's illness, that it's my mom who might die. "So it's not true."

"Nope," Mable says.

"So why were you crying?"

"Because I feel bad. I feel like your dad made a mistake not telling you things and I just went along with it because it was either that or not be in your life as much as I have been. And now—now you're this woman . . ." Mable pushes back into her overly firm pillow to get a better look at me. "You're not grown up but you're damn close and you're still in the dark."

"I don't know what I would have been like if you and Dad told me everything right away. I mean, who can say if I'd be better adjusted today if I had the facts."

"The fact is, and it's the facts that matter most, that your dad loves you so much. And no, I'm not your mom, but I feel like you're . . . not my daughter but my little sister or—no, I guess just my niece that I'm really close with, if that makes sense."

I nod. "It makes sense. But—it's like . . ."

"I know," Mable interjects. "It's like *niece* isn't special enough."

"It doesn't connote closeness."

Mable laughs. "It doesn't *connote closeness*? You are so prep school. Why even go to college; you have the vocab now. No wait—forget that last part; of course you're going to college— go wherever they have the best cereal bar. Seriously. You'll get a great education anywhere, meet friends wherever you go, but only a select few colleges and universities have a truly broad spectrum of cereal."

"I'll make sure to remember that on my tours," I say. "Good professors? Check. Well-equipped campus? Check. Cap'n Crunch and Grape-Nuts? Check."

"What made you ask this all of a sudden?"

I stand up and pace around the room while we talk. "It wasn't really all of a sudden. When I was in London Arabella and my friends Keena and Fizzy—yes, I know I now have friends with weird names—they got into the whole maternal mystery thing and then I thought about it."

"What were your clues?"

"You were married to a guy named David, right? That's Dad's name . . ."

Mable rolls her eyes. "For my millisecond marriage I was Mrs. David Goodman."

"You were married to David Good-man?" I say making his name an adjective.

"Yes, he was good, but sadly the free-loving grass roots enviro-freak that he was made him determined to not only save the world but be king of it."

"What became of Mr. Goodman?" I ask and pour myself a cup of water. The flowers I bought for Mable have long since shriveled up, but she saved one by drying it upside down and taping it to the wall. I don't touch it for fear I'll crunch it by accident.

"He sold blended juice drinks out of that green van we had and after we split, he went to San Francisco to"—Mable holds up her fingers in a piece sign and mellows her voice—"to like start an organic juice company, man."

"Nice," I say. "I'm sure he found inner sanctuary."

"Or something," Mable says. "I have an old acoustic guitar of his I always meant to send back."

"The one that I used to strum as a kid—the one with that paisley strap?"

Mable nods. "What else—what Sherlock symptoms did you obsess over?"

"Well, Galadriel is her name, right? And I only recently found out that your middle name starts with a G and . . ."

"Gina. My middle name is Gina. I went through a phase of using Gina as my first name but then . . . Worst nickname I ever had was in college when these cooler than thou mean kids called me Vag."

I crack up. "That's bad."

"Okay, Pukeowski—don't rub it in."

"Plus, it just seemed feasible. Like you and my dad made this pact to raise me apart but together and when I got old enough you'd . . ."

The big window that forms one of the room's walls is slightly tinted, so when the rain starts outside, the droplets appear gray, splattering random patterns of lines and dots on the pane.

Mable pats the bed so I'll come back over and sit next to her. It's very air-conditioned, so I get a blanket from the hallway and wrap it around my legs and tuck Mable in so she stays warm.

"Galadriel was my best friend," Mable says and picks at the bandage tape on her arm until I nudge her to stop. "We met at Sarah Lawrence College freshman year. She was this very cool, very dramatic woman. You know, a little like Arabella— how she can wear a cowboy hat and not look like an ass and then the next day be all into the downtown art scene. She always knew what was going on, even at eighteen she just had it."

"You mean that *it* that people talk about when they do bios of famous people?"

"Exactly. She made heads turn; she attracted people not just because she was gorgeous, but because she had this quality of . . ."

"Of what?"

"You know what it was? I've thought a lot about this over the years. It was that she wasn't ever there completely. Like she was just out of reach all the time, so it made you want to hear everything she said and know where she was headed next."

"If you know someone's going to leave, you want them more?" I take the blanket off my legs and put it on like a cape.

"So one spring break I brought her home. She was supposed to be in some movie filming in New York."

"She acted?"

"Not really—she was more in the right place at the right time all the time—all the time. So you'd say, Gala, where're you going after class? And instead of saying to the library to study or out for coffee, she'd say really casually that she was taking *insert name of big rock star here* to that guy in the village who customizes boots. And while she was there she'd bump into a pre-famous Julia Roberts and have coffee with her, and two years later Julia would ask Gala to come to a premiere, and so on . . . She was just one of those kinds of people who always seems to be on the pulse of everything."

"She sounds kind of cool—in that way," I say. "I don't want to be impressed with that stardom element, but I kind of am . . ."

Mable shakes her head. "Of course—of course it's cool. But it's not real. It's not a substitute for commitment and I just hope you know that."

"No—I get it. I get that knowing people and having *it* isn't everything . . . I have a clear picture of her, now," I say. "But it's so bizarre."

"No—here's a clear picture of her." Mable points to her closet and points me toward her blue suitcase in which there are extra clothes, a couple of books, and more papers and photos. She opens one of the books to its middle and hands me the photograph. "That's me and Galadriel. Gala—she was mainly called Gala."

"How old is she here?" I ask.

"That was freshman year of college, so just a little older than you are right now."

I'm staring at a picture of a woman who could be me, but with a more gleeful expression than I am prone to having plastered to my face. Same hair, same eyes, same wide cheeks, but somehow on her they manage to make her look sullen in a cool way rather than slightly moody. She is the kind of girl who looks pretty enough in a photo but can either be average when you meet her if she's got a boring personality or incredibly attractive if she makes you laugh.

"I must be a huge reminder of her all the time for my dad. And for you," I say.

"And this"—Mable pulls out another picture—"is Gala right before you were born."

"Maternity clothes are so much better now—she's all but wearing a muumuu here."

"She loved being pregnant. She ate eggplant all the time."

"I hate eggplant," I say as though this means something.

But everything's feeling like it means something. "Is my dad going to freak out that I know this stuff?"

"Probably. No—I'm not sure. I figured that he knew I was dribbling bits in now and then but he's got to know that you're an adult—sort of—and that you have a right to know your history, your familial past and present."

I lick my lips and push my hair away from my face. "Speaking of the present . . ."

"No—I don't speak with her. The chronology was this: She gave birth . . . no wait, before that, she met your dad over that spring break and they got together right away. Even though she was the Queen of Cool and he was this academic in button-downs and boat shoes, she just couldn't get enough of him. And he thought she was so wild and fun but with this softer side, too. They spent that summer living at the Vineyard . . ."

"At the cottage?"

"Yeah—your mother bought it. Right then. She just plunked down cash she had from various movies and odd jobs and they were all but married."

"Did they actually get married?"

"They did—not for a year or so, but then Gala dropped out of college and I kept going and I'd come back to Massachusetts or Rhode Island or wherever they were, and each time she was just a little less wild, a little less funny, a tiny bit more unhappy."

"So where do I fit into this?"

"So . . . suddenly it's the late eighties and the academic market is really tight and your dad's taking whatever position he can, and Gala's trying to do some business that was way ahead of its time—I can't remember the name but she'd customize tape covers and albums and when CDs hit, she somehow got linked back up with a couple of bands and helped produce a single that sold really well."

"And Dad?"

"I was a pastry chef at this fancy place in Back Bay then and I would go to the Flower Market to get edible flowers for the desserts—it was very over-the-top cuisine. So your dad came with me at one point and he was upset, saying that he thought Galadriel was miserable and had sort of lost her light. That was the expression he used. Lost her light."

"And then? Did he try to help her—or what made the light go off, did he say?"

"Sorry—I don't know all the details. I hung out with them but not much. She was already pulling away by then and I think I was this symbol of what she'd lost or given up by marrying and leaving school."

"So then what happened?" It's riveting and yet bizarre because it's hearing the story of pre-me but it feels like Mable's relating the plot of a movie or an ongoing drama that is actually real.

"Gala came by to see me at the restaurant and ate this eggplant puree we had in the walk-in fridge and, since she usually thought eggplants were the food equivalent of slugs, she knew she was pregnant. Fast forward to nine months later and your dad's arranged his cozy world—Gala staying at home with you, this newborn with tufts of bright red hair sprouting off only the sides of your head, not the top—you looked like a funny, tiny bald man . . ."

"Nice. So, let me guess. She tried being home with me, but after a couple years she just couldn't do it anymore and left?"

Mable sighs and bites her cuticles. "Um, I'm torn here. The next part is . . ."

"The leaving part."

"Right. Are you sure you want to know?"

I nod. "It's better for me to just deal with reality, isn't that what you were saying a couple weeks ago? That I need to be involved in my life?"

"I didn't really mean this. I meant more like take control of your day to day . . . . but okay." Mable reaches for a cup of water and takes a sip. "It wasn't a couple of years after you were born."

"Months?" I ask. "I'm trying to imagine the photo image of Gala springing to life, cradling a baby, but I can't."

"Neither could she. She left before Thanksgiving of that year."

I count on my fingers, feeling mathematically stunted at the moment. "So I was six weeks old?"

Mable nods. "She asked your dad to get up and give you a bottle—you can ask him about that—and when he came back to bed with it all warmed up, she was gone. They'd been to London that summer and she'd bought this huge brown suitcase and that was gone, so your dad knew right away. He also knew she was miserable but couldn't help her. He smothered her; he just wouldn't let her be; he was always trying to change her."

"That's interesting, because one of the things I think he's best at in terms of being a dad is that he doesn't really ask for change. He pretty much accepts me for who I am and isn't always pressuring me to conform."

"To his credit, David Bukowski was and is—from the minute you arrived in this world—an amazing father. He was the one who changed you. He was the one who strolled you around the neighborhood and talked to you like you understood everything and encouraged you to have an opinion."

"That was it? Never a word?"

"Your dad had some mental timeline. He left everything of hers as it was until exactly New Year's—he figured if she'd be back it'd be to celebrate a new year together. And when she didn't return, he boxed everything up and shoved away the clothing, the music, the pictures, all of it. And decided the best thing for you—who knew nothing of all this—was to just be a team together."

"With you on the side?"

"Yeah," Mable sighs. "Oh dear, I am so tired now."

I look at my watch. "We've been talking for hours."

"I know," Mable says, her eyes closed. "But it was about time."

Mable starts to drift off; I can tell by her breathing and her hands relaxing on the blanket. Outside, the rain has stopped and the sunshine is that really powerful bright kind you get in late spring. Is it late spring now or early summer? A small distinction. Did she leave me in good hands or desert me? Another distinction. I don't feel altered; I don't feel better or worse, just more informed.

I clean up the room a little so Mable won't wake to a mess, fold the blanket up and put it on the foot of her bed, and quietly walk to the door.

"Love," Mable calls, her voice sleepy, "ask your dad about your name."

"Okay," I say and then, with a sudden feeling of finality, I go back in and touch Mable's hand. "I'll see you soon?" What if Mable is telling me all this because she knows she's not going to be here later?

"Go for a run or something to clear your mind."

"I'm having dinner with my dad—again. I'm not sure he'll let me go running without him."

"He'll ease up—he's just scared." Mable opens her eyes and looks at me, then looks out the window. "Say hi to the world for me, okay?"

"I will. Actually, I'll run with Louisa. At least that gets Dad off my back. She and I are big cardio buddies now . . . I'll see you soon, right?" She nods and I kiss her cheek and let her sleep.

Chapter 10

"Whatever the fastest way is," I say to the post office worker and pay way too much to get my video project sent over in time for the deadline. It's not perfect; it's not even great, but it's good. Or at least it feels that way to me. Dad and I watched it a few nights ago and he cried and laughed along with Mable and gave a little cheer when he saw us walking all together. It was a nice break in the building tension between me and my father. Rather than little flare-ups that used to happen if I left my dishes in the sink or forgot to turn the heat down, the disagreements don't fade. He seems annoyed that I went to London, annoyed that I came back, just frustrated in general. So watching the video was good distraction. Louisa came over for the last few minutes—I think she didn't want to intrude—and brought us logs of chèvre, as if goat cheese had any relevance to the documentary whatsoever. But still, I'm not one to pass up cheese.

"Well, it's out of your hands now," Chris says, "just like love is out of mine."

"Oh will you stop being so dramatic. You're going to see Alistair in less than a month," I say and hold open the door for him.

"It feels like an eternity," Chris says. We walk from the small Beacon Hill post office to the Charles/MGH T stop so Chris can head to Cambridge for his Harvard tour. "Am I bumming you out with all this talk of my boyfriend when you are brokenhearted and single?"

"Did you ask that just so you could refer to Alistair as your boyfriend?"

Chris nods and smiles. "Pretty much, yeah. But are you okay or are you wallowing?"

"It varies per day—one minute I feel like I want to fly over and see him and rekindle or kindle since we hardly had the time together to justify a rekindling"—we lean on the concrete pillar near the stairs that lead to the train—"but other days it's all just so far removed from my life here, that is doesn't really matter. Does that make sense?"

"It does, actually. But you're allowed to feel bad about it— I mean you did almost love the guy and you did almost . . ."

"But I didn't. So . . ."

"So," Chris says, his voice changing tones completely, "are you sure you won't come with me?"

"I have no desire to parade around Harvard with you asking questions about their course requirements and the ratio of teachers to students and so on." Then I remember what Mable said. "But tell me what the cereal selection's like."

"You're twisted." Chris shakes his head. "How do I look? Collegial?" He fixes the collar on his shirt and I pick a fleck of lint from his shoulder.

"You look stunning, dahling," I say, affecting old-time Cary Grant. "They'd be silly fools not to let you in this instant."

"Slow down there, Mum; I don't even know if I'll get in. It is in the category of reach on my SIBOF sheet."

"SIBOF can bite my ass, I swear," I say.

"That sounds like an album name," Chris says and checks out some guy who walks by with a Harvard backpack.

"Oh, you're so in love you just have to ogle the other men . . . ," I taunt.

Chris defends himself with, "Hey—I'm allowed to look and who knows—that kid could be in my class at Haaahh-vard."

"Good luck," I say and reach for my cell phone because I have that phantom ringing thing where you think it's going to bleep at you but then it doesn't and you double-check just to make sure you didn't miss something.

Chris walks off and I dawdle along Charles Street, looking in the shop windows and the hardware shop that is set up so nicely it leaves me wishing I had a reason to purchase a shiny red wheelbarrow. But I don't. My hands feel empty after carrying the package of my final essays and video that we had to have converted to play in England. The only thing left hanging over me aside from my college tour and applications (of course, I can't apply without knowing where I want to go, so right now I'm stuck) is my "writing of the self." In my mind I go over the most recent email from Poppy Massa-Tonclair in which she stated:

> While I am sure your arrival back to the States hasn't
> been entirely smooth, please know that I am capable of
> extending the project only so far.

She didn't specify how far, whether meaning forever, or just until the LADAM year ends, which is around now, or if I can work on this thing over the summer.

I'm in front of one of the posh baby stores where they sell expensive booties and cashmere blankets when my cell phone really beeps. Chris programmed in the most obnoxious ring he could find, so the sound of a human voice saying *Get Off Yer Ass and Pick up the Phone* comes from my back pocket, causing two old ladies walking by to give me a look that suggests I should not be allowed out in public with my ass blaring.

"Hey!" Arabella says.

"Hey—listen, my phone bill was terrible—the international calls aren't included in my minutes. Let me call you when I get home?" I say and walk back down Charles Street toward Mass General.

"Oh, well, um I'm not actually . . ."

"Bels, I want to talk but I can seriously hear the dollars flying out the window and I don't want to start the summer entirely without cash."

"I know, it's just . . ."

"Talk later?" I say and hurry her off the phone. Maybe she had news of Toby and his noncheating on Nevis. Or maybe she saw Asher again and he confessed his love—she did say he told her he "made a mistake", so maybe he's ready to try again.

Would I be? Not sure. I don't want a relationship to be just a series of visits and emails. So maybe he's right. Or maybe I'm just justifying.

My phone rings again.

"I really can't talk right now," I say, assuming it's Arabella.

"Oh, sorry, Love," says a woman. "It's Louisa."

"No, I'm sorry . . . I didn't know it would be you. I was . . . never mind." I haven't spoken with her enough on the phone to recognize her voice right away.

"Listen, your dad asked me to call. He's with your aunt right now and didn't want to tie up her room phone, but I think you should go over there now if you can."

The street stops. The cars go by, beeping and noisy as before, but I don't hear them. I know why she's calling. Dad didn't want to call because he knew I'd hear it in his voice. "This is it, isn't it?" I ask.

"I think you should just come here," Louisa says.

Surprisingly, I don't cry, I'm just kind of numb and on automatic, walking past the stationery store, past the liquor store with its dusty bottles of expensive champagne in the window, under the overpass and across the busy street to the hospital area.

I watch a mom carrying her newborn outside. Next to her, a dad has a car seat, waiting for the mom to put the baby in it. The mom is holding so tightly and seems to be so wrapped up in the moment that the dad doesn't talk. They both just stand there looking at the baby. Did my mother look at me in my crib before she left? Did she ask my dad to get the bottle ready for me so she had time to change or did she steal that last couple of minutes alone with me?

I head inside the revolving doors and take the very familiar route to Mable's room. I get there, prepared to see my dad kneeling by her bedside or talking with doctors but instead, the room is empty. Trying not to think the worst, I rush to the nurses' station and ask.

"Your father took her to the sitting area."

In the muted beige and maroon tones of the waiting room I see my father's back and head, Mable's small frame wrapped in her terry cloth robe, and . . . rather than bad news and tears, I see Louisa grinning at me as I find them:

"Arabella," I say and "what the fuck" almost slips out but I catch it at, "What the . . ."

"I know! That's what I meant to get across to you on the phone—that this was a local call."

She and I hug and I say into her ear, "You have no idea how glad I am to see you—seriously. I am losing my mind."

She hugs me tightly, then says, "Someone thought it might be good for me to come over early—and what was I doing, really, anyway except packing and repacking."

I look at Mable. "Was this your idea? Thank you."

Mable shakes her head. "It wasn't me—thank him. And Louisa." She thumbs to my dad.

"I might be overbearing at times but I still have a little spontaneity left in me." He waits for me to object and say he's full of ideas and a real free spirit, but I don't. I might have before—when I was younger and thought he was—but not

now. Dad looks at me, knowing neither of us believes he's Mr.
Spontaneous. "You can thank Louisa."

"Thanks, Dad," I say and give him a real smigh—a
smile/sigh combo that means he did a good thing, even if it
wasn't his idea. "And thanks to you, Louisa." She nods at me
and doesn't make me hug her, for which I'm grateful. She and
I have an unspoken understanding—it's actually kind of nice. I
sit on the coffee table in front of my dad, Louisa, and Mable,
and Arabella is cross-legged on the couch next to us.

"Why don't you take Arabella back to the house—I'm sure
she's exhausted," Dad says and it's not so much an ask but a tell.

"I thought we were hanging out here," I say and watch
Mable's face to see if she wants me to stay or to leave.

"I have some things to talk to your dad about," Mable says,
"and then I need to rest. It took the better part of an hour to
get from my bed to here." She tries to make a joke of it but the
truth is obvious to everyone: She is weak and frail and thin.

"Shall we?" Arabella asks.

I nod and help her get her bags. "This is it?" I heft a can-
vas shoulder bag. Arabella carries a small duffel. "You only have
this and that?"

"Are you mad, woman? I couldn't possibly fit three months
worth of clothing into these bags. The rest is arriving directly
at the Vineyard."

"And here I was so impressed with your newfound sim-
plicity," I say as we wait for the elevator.

"You can take the girl away from Monti's enormous closet,
but you can't take the closet out of the girl . . ."

"My car is all the way at the other end of Charles Street. Do you mind walking the whole way?" I ask as we go out the revolving doors. The couple with the newborn baby is gone, but other moms and dads and families stand with their kids, and I watch the cycle of it, the leaving, the going, the pausing for air, the way families and friends overlap.

"Dear girl, I'm English—we walk for miles without complaining." Arabella gives a haughty toss of her unbrushed hair and then adds, "But I need to change my shoes first. I didn't realize it would be so warm here."

Cut to later that evening when Arabella is deciding whether to dye her hair from a box or eat another goat yogurt (the fridge is filled with little pots of goat-gurt, courtesy of Louisa).

"Aren't they fairly divergent activities? One involves altering your physical self—and it's not a wash out, I have to remind you—it says on the box. Plus, wouldn't you just go to a hairdresser? Don't you have access to basically every hair guru in London?"

"As you know, I am a Daniel Galvin devotee. However, being away is like having an affair or something; it's so tempting to mess around." She paws at her locks and then reconsiders. "But, if I messed up, it's not like I can fly him in to fix it." I raise my eyebrows at her. "Well, he might fly in as a favor, but it wouldn't be cost-effective. Bring on the goat-gurt."

When I come back up with a goat-gurt in one hand (for her) and an orange Creamsicle in the other (for me), she's not in my room and not in the bathroom.

"I'm out here," she yells and I walk to the open window above my desk. "Bring out the gurt."

"Hang on," I say and make an attempt at getting out onto the roof without killing myself, dropping my icepop, or slopping yogurt down onto the ground. Once I'm outside with her, I wonder why it is I've never ventured out here.

"Because you always do what you're meant to do," she says and spoons her dairy product into her mouth.

"Not always," I say. "It's habit. Or it's instinctual. Some people have that trait where they don't care or they don't worry, but even if I try to be nonchalant I can't help it. I'm the opposite."

"You're chalant?"

"Exactly. Now give me a break and let me enjoy my Popsicle before it melts."

We lie back on the sheet Arabella brought out to cover the hot roof shingles. Distant noise from campus doesn't distract us from our key place up above the fields, the chairs that have been brought out from storage in preparation for graduation in a couple of weeks, the shorts-and-tank-top-clad masses.

Arabella finishes her snack and stretches out in full beach goddess mode, despite the sinking sun, and removes her T-shirt to reveal a patterned bra. "I figured if it's floral it could pass as a bikini," she says.

"Well, don't wear it on campus—you can't wear bikinis or tankinis . . ."

"Or drink martinis . . ."

"Basically, no inis anywhere near campus."

"Got it," Arabella says. "What about you, are you beach-ready?"

"Café-ready, you mean? I guess. I don't really know when to go, though."

"Well, I've been instructed to head down for Memorial Day to set up. I guess we'll have limited service from then until sometime in early June?"

I can feel the skin on my arms pinking up and sit up so I can either get sunblock or go inside. "Right—after graduation."

"Why, are you sticking around for graduation?"

"I assumed I would but I guess I don't really have to . . ."

"What about those parties you told me about—like the one on the beach when you and Jacob had that misunderstanding?"

"Ah, ballistic at Crescent Beach. Good times."

Arabella shields her eyes from the sun and turns her face toward me. "Maybe you should go—you're always saying you should get out more, have more fun . . ."

"Yeah, but who's to say senior parties are where the fun is?"

"Who's to say they're not?" Arabella says and then goes back to sunning herself. "You have to join me—I'm in full summer mode here. What's stopping you?"

I put my chin in my hands and study the wisps of hair that fall into my eyes. "I don't really know what I'm waiting for," I say and head inside before I get royally spf-ed at my own fair skin and muddled brain.

Chapter 11

In the middle of the night I awake to a nearly full moon and a completely full head. Not full of myself in the conceited "aren't I so great" way, and not in the "head-cold-fuzzy, need some decongestant" way, but in the "oh my God, I just came to a stunning realization about my life" way that you think will result in a huge epiphany but instead just leads to more confusion.

Arabella sleeps in her traditional "head under the covers unaware of anything else except her" dormant delirium, so I don't feel guilty when I turn on the light and start sketching out my full plans in my journal. It's time for me to make a plan. I always feel better when I know what I'm doing next.

I spend the next hour on the roof, looking at the stars and looking at my minimap of America's colleges to see if any of the color-coded by region states and their places of higher learning suddenly call out to me. I even close my eyes, turn the map all around, and point to see if by tempting fate I am handed answers. But to no avail.

"Forget it," I say to no one but the clear night sky. I'll go on my college visits later in the summer; there's no way I could focus on it now. So basically I'm up on the roof with no better sense of what I'm doing, literally half inside my room and half in the window with my journal tucked under my arm. I look at my clock: It's the middle of the night here but eight o'clock in the morning in England, so I throw caution and magazine-style advice to the wind and decide to call Asher.

"Hi, darling," he says when he picks up the phone.

"Hi," I say and then it hits me that he doesn't have caller ID or anything and why would he pick up the phone with such an overt greeting. "It's Love."

"Right! I know that—of course. I can still recognize your voice, you know; it hasn't been that long . . ."

It hasn't, I want to say, but it feels like it. But I go for the benign, "I was just calling to say hi." Um, which I already did.

"Oh, hi."

Silence. Bad idea #1. "So," I say, "did I wake you?"

"Ah, no. I've been up for a bit . . . just sorting out some festival formalities, registering, and—well, I won't bother you with the details."

The thing is, I like being bothered with the details. Details are what make life exciting and make you really know someone. But I guess after you break up you don't know those details anymore, those specifics that mean that you're the one he calls or she's the one you think about telling that funny conversation to. "You can always bother me with details," I say.

"Thanks, I'll remember that. Isn't it the middle of the night where you are?"

Where I am sounds so vague—as though he can't even remember my town or the fact that he was going to visit me. "It
is. Your sister's asleep in my room but I woke up for some reason and can't get back to sleep."

"Did you try warm milk?"

"What?"

"Warm milk—it's meant to be soothing or something. That
or a couple shots of hard liquor."

"I think I'll pass on both, thanks." I can hear a doorbell
chime in the background and suddenly it feels like I'm wast-
ing his time. "I should let you go." Or rather, we have let each
other go.

"Love—before you hang up . . . it's. I'm. I'm really sorry I
hurt you."

I hate that he feels some sort of power there, even if it's a
little true—that he hurt me but I did nothing but sit there pas-
sively being dumped. "It wasn't you really, Asher. It was us—
the situation."

"Right, and if you'd been here or stayed or if you were
somehow English, the whole trouble wouldn't even have been
an issue."

I watch my brow furrow automatically in the mirror.
"Trouble? I don't see why you'd call it trouble?"

"Fine." Asher's tone changes a little and I can imagine his
cheeks flushing like he's gone running or is about to defend
himself. "I'll call it what it was—not trouble—the exact term
is cheating. Is that better?"

Cheating? Were we playing poker? What the hell is he talking about? I'm tempted to shove Arabella so she can wake up and listen and decipher for me but 1) she's way too heavy a sleeper and 2) she wants to be left out of all things Asher-related. "Define cheating," I say and feel my pulse pick up speed.

"I really don't want to get into all of this. I'm sure my sister's done a number on my bad behavior as it stands."

"Leave Arabella out of it, Asher. Just tell me in your own words what the real reason is that you aren't visiting here, that you broke up with me . . ." I think of Arabella telling me that Asher came by her flat and told her he'd "made a mistake." I thought then that he meant he'd been wrong to break up with me but now I think he meant he screwed up by cheating on me.

"Let me guess—that wacky and wonderful Valentine?" I spit out.

"I have to get the door," he says and his footsteps echo. "Listen, I wasn't up for long distance anyway, okay? And with you not here and a couple of drinks and . . . Valentine's not the issue here."

"No, you're right. She's not. Your asinine behavior, your totally shoddy decision-making skills are. At the time, all your impulsivity was so charming. So endearing. But now I see it was just a ruse. What was I, just some cute American conquest you failed to have?"

"It wasn't like that and you know it, Love. If you want to belittle our relationship, that's your choice. I can't stop you."

"And I can't stop you from doing whatever it is you're

doing. It makes me wish I'd spent more time with Nick Cooper."

"Nick Cooper? What does he have to do with anything?"

"Nothing. Nothing—never mind. Just forget it. Forget me."

"Don't end it like this, Love—please . . . ," Asher says quietly, the words slightly muffled as when you don't want the other person who's in the room to hear you.

I humph loudly, "Don't tell me she's there? She's actually in the room with you? Gross. I have to go." I shake my head, angry at him, at myself, at my continual naïveté or selective viewage of the opposite gender. Maybe I should major in gender studies like Chris wants to so I can anthropologize my own stupid behavior. Robinson Hall cheated on me, now Asher Piece. Will this be one of those patterns you see on TV and fifteen years from now I'll be either lecturing on my poor picking of dates or have a successful turnaround and can motivationally speak about it. . . .

"Good luck with your new girlfriend," I say.

"She's not my girlfriend," he says.

"Fine. Good luck with your nongirlfriend. And do me a favor. If I ever come to London and am tempted to look you up or we see each other at Arabella's wedding in ten years, leave me alone."

"Love, I . . ."

Click. Power returned to me at least momentarily by hanging up. Another transatlantic transmission call that has left me a couple dollars poorer and a whole lot more full of angst.

I don't know exactly what I wanted from that phone call, but the details of his infidelity were not on the list of possibil-ities. The only plus side is that it makes me miss him less and makes it a tiny bit easier to cut ties. Won't be wearing the white turtleneck that I was wearing when I met him anytime soon. I wonder how I'll feel when it's winter and I'm a senior and go to pull that shirt out: Will I remember meeting him in the topiary garden and feel sad, or will I put it on without thinking about it? Maybe distance helps placate the wounds but the tangible things still remain—the shirts, the mixes, the little presents acquired. No wonder my dad boxed up all of Gala's stuff when he realized she wasn't coming back—who could live in the constant debris of memories and missing?

As quietly as I can, I get dressed, slip (not literally, though I wouldn't put it past my nongraceful self) down the stairs, and after leaving a note for Dad and Bels saying I went to see her, I get into the car and drive to see Mable.

Of course, it's after hours and you can't just expect to visit the hospital just because it's now four-forty-five in the morn-ing and you're awake. However, when I get to the front desk they let me in, and when I reach the nurses' station, they tell me Mable's been asking for me.

Wordlessly, I kiss Mable's cheek. Her skin is papery thin now as though she's been flattened; maybe she has been. Mable's eyes flutter and she stirs.

"They told me I could come in, sorry," I whisper.

"No, no, don't be sorry, I wanted you here," she says. She turns to look out the window. "Hello, world."

"Want me to help you over there?"

Mable nods. "Yeah, but I don't think I can. It's been a tough couple of days."

I gulp and feel that familiar worry swirling in my body, but I know that's not what she needs right now. "I could wheel you over there," I suggest.

"Yeah—just put up the rail here and unclick that thingy." She points to the wheels on her bed.

I roll the bed closer to the window, not caring if I'll get in trouble with the doctors. The process takes a few minutes since we have to roll the IV stand, too, and the pulse monitor comes off, which sends a nurse in. She's about to object when I plead with her using my eyes, which probably look very sad right about now. The nurse nods and says she'll be back in a minute to help move the bed back.

I sit next to Mable on her bed, both of us looking out the window at the earliest morning light. Below, the skyline of Boston shines.

I point to the glowing Citgo sign. "That reminds me of my first time at Fenway with you. You let me have three hot dogs."

"I knew you'd either love me for it or feel sick and learn your lesson."

"Both," I say.

She points to another place. "Remember the pedicures on Newbury Street?"

"And the mean girls you told me to ignore. You were right—it's not really worth it to buy into the girl cat fighting fiasco."

"Glad to be of service. Hey, look, you can kind of—suspend your disbelief with me here—see the corner where Slave to the Grind is."

I sigh. "God, I had so many nights there—Chinese food with you, bemoaning my lack of love life or latteing myself into a frenzy over work—stopping there after I did those voice-overs . . ."

Mable pokes my leg. "You should do those again—you liked that."

I shrug. "I don't know." Then I remember something. "I did get an offer from Martin Eisenstein to look him up if I'm ever in LA . . ."

"Holy crap—really? Well, you get your butt out there and see what he has to offer you—oh, but if it's skeezy and involves dating him or something, come right back."

"I don't think I'm heading to California anytime soon," I say. "I might not go anywhere."

Mable turns to me and stops looking at the bright lights outside. "We had a lot of great days together."

"You're speaking in the past tense and it's scaring me."

Mable doesn't comfort me or shake off my observation. "And you have to remember great days, you have to catalog them—in your mind or in your journal. Because it's the shitty days that seem to cluster and accumulate and the great ones only stand out for a moment."

I nod, letting the tears fall, with the line *days glowing like a firefly and then fading out* from a song I once wrote in my journal floating in my mind.

• • •

"Ahhh!" Mable lets out an angry roar. "I wish I could just re-arrange the atoms in my body."

"So you'd be well?" I ask.

"No, I meant so I could slip out the window and float around." She swings her hand toward the window. "So I could revisit all the places from my great memories." She puts her head back on the pillow. "But I can't."

"You look really tired," I say.

"I am." She nods. "Listen, Love . . . tell me something you've never told me before."

"Why?"

"So this day—this moment can be a good memory, not a terrible one—so you can think about it afterward and feel more than just sorrow."

I think but can't find any untold information that feels worthy of right now. "You go first, Aunt Mable."

"So . . . Mable isn't my real name," she says. Again, I have that tiny flick of wonder if she'll announce her real name is Galadriel.

"So what is it?" I ask and hold both of her hands in mine.

"My name is really 'Maybelline.'"

I laugh. "I can't believe you're named after a mascara."

Mable laughs back, her trademark cackle. "No, not the mascara, the song, 'Maybelline.'"

"I don't know it," I say.

"Come on—you, collector of classics, maker of mixes?" I shake my head and Mable says, "I'll put it on a disk for you."

"Deal," I say. "Then I can sing it for you."

"Don't think you're getting out of telling me something I don't know about you . . . fair is fair."

"This isn't fair," I say and start sobbing. I feel certain I won't see her again and I know she's thinking the same thing.

"I know it's not. And there's nothing I can do to make it fair except to tell you I love you and that living means keeping going."

"Like Dylan said?"

Mable nods. "Yeah, keep on keeping on. But—tell me your thing."

Squeezing her hands but not looking at her because it just hurts too much, I say, "The thing you don't know is that . . . is that it doesn't matter that Galadriel gave birth to me. Because the truth is, you're my mom anyway, right? You're the one who told me about love and boys and how to respect myself. You're the one who made me write down the songs in my head."

Mable cries and cries and I lie on her chest, ignoring the tubes and awkward position my back is in and that it might be painful for her to bear my weight. "When they ask me on these college essays and interviews *who's the person who influenced you most,* I'll say you."

It takes every ounce of strength I have or have ever had, to get up from the bed, kiss and hug her, and leave. But she asks me to leave her there, and when I go to the nurses' station to get them to move the bed back, I don't return to the room. I do

as Mable asked and go home to my father to tell him to come
see her. I drive and cry and wonder at the speed of years and
days, how fast the present happens and how quickly what
you're going through changes from the right now into a memory.

Chapter 12

What no one tells you about funerals, about people really dying, is that nothing really changes. You still have to get dressed and brush your hair and sleep and eat and pee but all the while knowing that there's this loss out there, this unchangeable thing lurking beneath every action, every thought.

I sit with my dad at the front of the Hadley Hall chapel and pat his hand. He gave a good speech and seems to be doing—considering the circumstances—okay. We're both "okay." Louisa has been the one to help organize the food and flowers, the one who helped make the phone calls bearing bad news.

At the back of the chapel, my friends are sitting, showing their support. Not tons, but the close ones—Arabella, Harriet Walters, Chili Pomroy, and Chris. Even Lila Lawrence came up from Newport. Faculty members such as Mr. Chaucer and Lana Gabovitch keep to themselves but nod hello. Miles, Mable's ex-fiancé, said hello to me and started to say something else but we didn't have time to talk before the service started with its heavy chords and organ music, which Mable would have hated.

Back at our house, the downstairs is a mass of mourning, plat-
ters of crackers and cheese, deli meats for those of us who feel the
need to stifle our sadness with salty snacks and tepid lemonade.
Dad is in his study, momentarily escaping the crowd of coffee
people, Mable's old friends from her past jobs and school, and I'm
on the spiral staircase, sitting in my all-black attire.

"Mable would hate that I'm so typically funereal," I say and
pluck the dark linen of my trousers up, then let it fall.

"But she'd like what you said," Chris points out.

"It was just stuff from my journal," I say and shrug. I'm all
cried out right now, more stunned and tired. I give a quick visual sweep of the room to see if Miles is here, but he's not. He
must have left.

"You always talk about it like it's drivel," Jacob says from his
place to my left. I look at him through the slats of the banis-
ter. "But as far as I can tell, your journal is pretty incredible."

Chris gives me just the tiniest nudge, subtle enough so I get
that he heard what Jacob said but not enough so that everyone
gets Chris's point.

"Love—I'm really sorry," Lila says. She's still a walking
Golden Globe, all legs and streaks of blond and already toasty
tan on her way out to "Cali for vacay" as she phrased it. "I have
to go—my flight's tomorrow and I haven't even packed."

Arabella is on the other side of the room, helping serve
food and clear drinks and, though it goes unsaid, staying away
from Lila Lawrence. The fact that they both slept with the
same guy draws an invisible line between them that neither
one wants to acknowledge.

• • •

Later, when the house has emptied and Arabella and I have finished the dishes, I go into the living room to help put the furniture back in place. Dad hefts the couch a few feet back and
I take a side table over to where it belongs near the big floral
chair.

"It's so weird, Dad. I feel like calling someone to talk about
this whole day—you know, describe the event and everything . . ."

"But let me guess, the person you'd call is Mable?" Dad sits
on the couch and surveys the clean room.

"Yeah," I sigh and sit next to him. On my way I move a
vase of flowers over to the table and as I do, I notice that there's
an arrangement that doesn't match the others.

"I'm turning in," he says. "Louisa's staying the night if that's
okay with you."

I turn to him. "You don't have to clear it with me."

"You live here, I live here; I just want you to have a voice,"
he says. "I'm beat—and I have my graduation introductions to
write."

Graduation. Parents traipsing all over campus. End of the
year. "Do you need me to stick around? I mean, Arabella's
going to the Vineyard . . ."

Dad stops in his tracks. "Well, not that this is the most ap-
propriate time to discuss this—but . . . we have a couple of
things to sort out."

"Are you canceling it?"

Dad shakes his head. "No, Mable made me promise to let

you and Arabella go. She's already got Ula and Doug set and the property's paid up for a year, and if it winds up being successful, she has a potential buyer."

"Who?"

"Whom. Trip Randall. The man who owns it."

Henry's dad. Mr. Uptight Blazer and Cocktails at Noon himself. "He wants to buy Slave to the Grind?"

Dad swallows and flaps his hand—his gesture for let's drop this. "This doesn't really concern you. It's just business, part of Mable's estate planning."

"Okay—I mean, I'd like to be involved. I know I'm a minor but only until this fall, so you can tell me things. I'm competent . . . ," I say. I go back to the little flower arrangement and study it. The outside is all green and the flowers are all lily of the valley. "These are out of season," I say.

"I didn't get them—I wouldn't know the first thing about flowers," Dad says.

"These are Mable's favorite." Were, I think. They were her favorite. "Did Miles send them?" Mable's ex-fiancé is the only one I can think of who would have known and found her favorite flowers. They must have been imported and expensive to find at this time of year. Then, stuck to the bottom of the circular glass vase, I see a small note card. It reads;

from your old friend, G. Together in spirit.

Without showing my shock to my father, it clicks that they are from Galadriel. Gala. She's out there in this world, somewhere, which I guess I knew but it is stunningly odd to feel it hit home.

"You can go to the Vineyard after your work is completed," Dad says. "After you have final approval from your overseas professors and after . . ."

"After what?" I ask. The school stuff makes sense, so there's not much point in arguing for shoving off tomorrow, like Arabella is.

Dad reconsiders something. "You know what? Nothing. We can talk more this weekend, okay?"

"Okay," I say and we hug for a while in the quiet early-summer night.

Chapter 13

"**A**re you sure you'll be okay?" I ask Arabella for the hundredth time.

"You're not really expecting me to answer you again, are you? Listen, I've got it all sorted." She flaunts her bus ticket to Wood's Hole and says, "Bus then ferry, then Ula and Doug will fetch me and bring me to the world of coffee. Hey—what about that for a name?"

"World of Coffee?" I ask and wrinkle my nose. "I don't think so—it sounds like a department store. It's not what Mable had in mind." I've been wrapped up in thinking about what Mable would have wanted—or did want—for her café, and for me, and I've come to the conclusion in the past twenty-four hours that she just wanted me to keep going. Like she said, keep on keeping on. But it's not easy.

"Are you still thinking about calling her?" Arabella shoves the last of her clothing into her shoulder bag and zips it closed. I nod. "When my grandpa died I remember that Angus actually went to the phone a whole bunch of times—he'd read an article in the Sunday papers and just felt the need to share it. But of course he couldn't."

"I'm narrating in my head to her as though she can hear me," I say. "And don't add something cheesy like—well, Love, she can hear you in spirit."

"I won't get sappy on you—but I do believe she is with us."

Dad knocks at the door and sticks his head into the room. "You better get going if you're going to make the bus—South Station is bound to be busy for the long weekend."

"Good advice, thanks, Dad," I say and when he closes the door I tell Arabella, "It was obvious advice but I'm trying to placate him with *good suggestion* and *great idea* so that he thinks I'm doing as I'm told and doesn't watch my every move. He used to be so much more mellow. A couple years ago I felt like there were hardly any rules."

"Maybe that's because you didn't need them," Arabella says.

I help her with her bag and we flip-flop down the spiral staircase and through the kitchen to the porch where Dad and Louisa are lounging outside. Dad's been spending only half days on campus and then working from home, taking calls in his study, writing his graduation introductions in the living room while I write in my journal. There are only a couple more pages left until it's totally full with all my words for the past two years. (Note to self: Buy new one prior to going to Martha's Vineyard.)

"I'll be back in a couple of hours," I say to my father.

He flops the section of newspaper he's reading down so it

rests on his chest and says, "Have a good trip down—and call when you get there, okay? I gave Doug and Ula your arrival time, so one of them will be there to meet the ferry. Look for the coffee car."

"Sorry—what?" I ask him.

Dad swallows and shakes his head, "The coffee car—it's one of those Smart Cars, those little fuel-efficient things. . . ."

"Let me guess—it's brown and it's supposed to look like a little roasted coffee bean?" I ask and can't help but smile when I give in to the mental image of swishing around town in a car that looks like it belongs in someone's toy chest.

Dad smiles and looks all poignant. "That's exactly what Mable pictured and that's how she told me to describe it to the place that customized it. When you decide on a name, it'll go on the side—one of those magnetized signs."

Arabella lifts her bags again, signaling me that we should go. "Sounds good. Be back soon."

"We can talk more when you get back, okay?" Dad holds his gaze on me a little longer than he normally does, telling me in that silent but stern parental way that we're due for a chat (chat=serious discussion).

"See you later," Louisa adds. She's been very quiet since the funeral, really staying in the background. I guess this is smart on her part—she probably is wary of stepping on our grieving toes. But part of me—the slightly paranoid way overanalytical part—thinks this is the prelude to "the talk" that Dad keeps mentioning. I'm sure he expects me to fall apart when they tell me they're moving in together. The truth is, she's here a lot anyway—and I've only got one more year before college and damned if I'm going to get in the way of my dad having a love life. That said, it feels a little bizarre to think of her moving her stuff in—and I know I'm ahead of myself here, but lately I've pictured trying to do the father-daughter stuff that we've always done and I feel sad that the team is breaking up.

I tell an abbreviated version of this to Arabella in the car as we attempt to get on the highway to the bus station. "Maybe you're not really losing the twosome," she says with her window rolled down and luxurious chestnut hair billowing in the breeze. "Maybe it's more like increasing your team. You know, like when a band gets a second guitarist or something."

I think for a minute and feel my nerves tense as the traffic slows to a full stop. "Bands always break up after they change like that, though." After we sit for fifteen minutes going nowhere, I decide to turn around.

"I should've taken the T," Arabella says. "Sorry."

"No—I don't care about the traffic; I just want you to get to the ferry." I make a plan and hand my cell phone to Arabella so I won't be diagnosed with the Talk n' Drive disease that plagues our nation. "I'm driving you to Wood's Hole. That way, we can hang out and sing and stop for French fries at Sam's and rush you to the boat in style."

Arabella takes her flip-flops off, slides her car seat back as far as it will go, and puts her bare feet on the glove compartment. "Bliss," she says and rolls her window down all the way as I take the next exit, reverse directions on the highway, and start heading south. "What should I do with the phone?"

"Oh—when we're past the halfway point, like around the Bourne Bridge, call my dad and tell him what we're doing."

"Why then?" she asks and starts to rummage around for music.

"So that he can't tell me to turn back. If we're more than halfway there, he'll feel compelled to let me keep going—it wouldn't make sense by then to turn around."

"Smart, Grasshopper, very smart."

"If I knew the sound grasshoppers made, I would do it right now," I say and smile.

"Creek creek?"

I shrug. "That's a cricket noise. Now, put in a disc and let's go."

A while later, I drive over the Bourne Bridge, admiring the view of the water and wishing I were going over with Arabella. "I'm just totally claustro," I say and sound whiny enough that I apologize out loud.

"You're allowed to whine and moan," Arabella says, "but it's not going to do any good. All you have to do is get through the next ten days and then—boom—summer will officially begin and we'll be all set."

"I know, you're right—and seeing as I am such the non sequitur queen right now—are you sure you're okay with my sleeping bag?"

"I've been camping before, Love—in the actual wilderness. Living in an unfurnished apartment should be fine." She pauses. "At least until you get down there."

"If worst comes to worst you can always sleep on a couch

in the café. Actually, that probably isn't the best idea. I'll get all the linens and pots and pans together and bring them next week, don't worry."

"Pots and pans? Who's planning on doing any cooking?" Arabella asks and isn't entirely joking. Maybe we've got different visions of the summer. This thought hits me suddenly and makes me worry.

"Um, it's called food and we'll need some sustenance if we're going to function."

"Can't we eat the café food?" Arabella asks.

I make a face that causes her to look at me like I'm a big bitch. "I think having the occasional scone is fine—but we can't exactly live off the baked goods. The place does have to make a profit."

Arabella looks out the window. "I know you're having a rough time—but once we're down there, I really hope you'll be able to relax."

"What's that's supposed to mean?" I ask and swing into the parking lot by the ferry terminal. Kids with Popsicles wander around, cars wait in line to drive onto the boat, and preppy people and their Labradoodles sit on the benches waiting for their long weekend to begin.

"It means that sometimes you take everything way too seriously. Live a little. What does Chris always say? Chill. Just be chill."

"I hate when people tell me to chill. I'm not wine. Whine, maybe."

Arabella gets her bags from the trunk and we hug good-bye. "I'm going to run in and get my ticket. You better get back to your dad."

"Have fun and let me know what else to bring—and keep me posted about the coffee creeps." After Doug and Ula brought a stack of overdue bills by the house and didn't even acknowledge her presence, Arabella started calling them the coffee creeps—or the CCs. She figures this is good code since I told her CC usually stands for Cape Cod around here.

"I'll be sure to give you a full report. And I'll keep my eye out for your SF."

I pull back and look at her. "What's that? Abbreviations I don't know? How ghastly."

"SF. Summer Fling."

I raise one eyebrow at her. "As long as you're sure the *F* is for fling."

She shrugs. "Depends what you're looking for—friend, flirt . . ."

"You can stop right there," I say. The ferry sounds its deep, loud horn and I wait with her bags while Arabella runs in to buy her ticket.

"Thanks for the ride, Jeeves!" she shouts from way up on the top deck. Seagulls careen and dive, looking for bread and fish, and I wave exaggeratedly from the shore from my post on the hood of the Saab.

I'm about to get back in the car, deal with traffic and turmoil by rushing back for my "chat" at home, but I consider what Arabella said. No one likes to be told they're uptight, and being fairly self-aware, I can own up to being farther down the stressy spectrum than I'd like. Mable always told me to mellow, and I seem to cultivate friends like Chris and Arabella who have a knack for leisure. Maybe this is my psyche's way of saying I need to find some of that, too.

So I sit on my car's hood, staring out at the ocean, and give myself a full ten minutes of Atlantic Zen before hunting for change so I can grab a snack from the vending machine. The snacks are held hostage for quarters, dimes, and nickels in one of those antique contraptions where you drop your money in, hope it registers, and pull a knob out and plead for your candy or chips to actually come out. I debate the merits of a Sugar Daddy—those overly sweet caramel pops that are desirable in part because of their suggestive name—and a bag of Fritos, possibly the saltiest corn product known to consumers. I decide to go for the Fritos and drop in my money, pull the sticky knob (note to self: Find hand-sanitizer back in the car), and the vending machine coughs up neither the chips I requested nor the candy I almost did.

"Tootsie Rolls?" I say out loud in my amazed stupor. Some kid next to me stands waiting for his turn. "Do you want Tootsie Rolls?"

"I want Fritos," he says.

"Well, so did I but apparently you don't get to choose." I pat the machine as though it's a burly dog. "Vendy here gets to pick for you—just so you know. Don't get your hopes up . . ."

I sit on the bench next to the machine and ponder my newfound sweets. Maybe they're an omen of some kind. Then a bag of Fritos is thrust in front of my downward face.

"Oh, you don't have to give me yours," I say, expecting to find the kid there but instead I'm squinting into the afternoon sunlight at:

"Charlie," he says, as though meeting me for the first time. "I notice you don't have any liquid products with you this time—glad to be out of the face of danger." But it's not the first time I've seen his incredible visage—handsome and just a little bit stubbled—he's already tan—no doubt from fishing and working outside all the time. There's something so appealing about him; he's rugged where Asher was polished. Not that I'm doing a point-by-point comparison, but Charlie's physique lends itself to description: the way his mouth curls up on one side, his lips full, the way he seems so comfortable, not that awkward stance so many guys have that makes it seem like they don't know where to put their hands or where to look next. Charlie looks right at me, then lets his eyes study my mouth.

I stand up so I won't be making that pinched eyebrows wrinkly nose face at him. "No frappés this time." I stick out my hand to shake his. "Love Bukowski—just in case you've forgotten. It's been a long time." I wonder if this gets across my pissy feelings at being stood up while not totally being so rude that he writes me off.

"It has," he says. "This is my little cousin, Drake."

"As in Nick Drake?" I ask and immediately think of Jacob and his love for said musician—guilt makes me blush. Though why I feel guilty I don't completely understand.

"I doubt it—though he is a great singer. Hey—Drake—

want some Tootsie Rolls?" Drake shrugs and chucks her Sugar
Daddy over, and I manage to catch it with my right hand (a
small feat being left-handed as I am) and seem vaguely together. "Drake's visiting for a few weeks."

"Visiting . . ."

"My family. On the island." Charlie pauses for a second.
"Are you heading down?"

I shake my head and think about unwrapping the Sugar
Daddy so I can eat it. Then I think maybe it'll look too porn—
like I'm being overtly sexual by licking the lollipop, so I refrain
from snacking. "I was dropping off a friend," I say and like that
I didn't clarify what kind of friend. Let him think it was a
boyfriend. I don't care.

"Oh," he says. "I was on standby but the truck didn't get
on." He points to his pickup off in the huddle of SUVs and
cars. "We'll make it on the next one."

I check my watch and my internal clock tells me I am way
overdue in getting on the road. "Well, I'll see you around."
Then I remember something. "What were you doing at Bartley's Burgers, anyway?"

Charlie grins. "Same thing as you—getting food."

"I meant . . ." I start but then stop. It's not really my business to know what he was doing in Cambridge.

"I know what you meant. I was just giving you a hard
time," he says and gives me his look again, where he stares a
fraction of a second too long and makes me shiver even
though it's warm outside.

"You like doing that, I think," I say. Hello, Flirty.

"You might be right," he says. "I was up taking care of some loose ends." I look at him, wishing he'd be more specific, but he interprets my look as disbelief. "I am allowed to go off Martha's Vineyard."

I laugh to hide my embarrassment. "I know that—of course you are. But . . . I don't know—it was weird seeing you there." I instantly think of having lunch there with Mable. "It's a place I sort of associate with my aunt." I stop talking and hope he'll finish the good-bye or change the subject.

"How is she, by the way?" Charlie asks then looks behind me at his cousin. "Drake—don't even think about getting something else—we're having a family dinner when we get there." I remember that Charlie said he wasn't close to his family, but maybe that's changed—or maybe he just meant the typical not always seeing eye-to-eye stuff that always slides in and out the familial window.

How is Mable? I've gone though imaginary conversations like this, where I have to pick a way to inform my conversant that Mable is gone, but here's my first time saying it in reality.

"Mable died, actually. Really recently." I nod a couple times and sigh. It's the best way to say it—the most direct and honest so I don't have to deal with overly sympathetic people or go into the whole story of her demise.

For a second, Charlie looks like he's going to step forward and hug me, which fills me with that pre-touch anticipation, but he doesn't. "She was really special," Charlie says. It's the first time someone hasn't started with "Sorry," and it feels better somehow.

"She was," I say, the past tense feeling—sadly—a little more normal each time I use it. "I do have to go, though."

"Me, too," Charlie says as the next boat sounds. "Maybe I'll see you later?"

"That's what you said before—and it proved true," I say.

"Maybe I'll look you up next time I come up to the big city," he says, putting on a Southern accent for the *big city* part, letting me know he's aware of his small town persona.

"You could do that," I say. And I'm just about to tell him that he doesn't have to wait until then, that I'm coming down to the Vineyard to live full-time for three months, when I remember waiting for him in that little diner. Waiting for a guy who never shows means that he's likely to pull that crap again—at least that's what Mable said—and for now I've got to trust her.

I stick out my hand so he'll shake it—both because I want to feel his skin on mine again, but also to protect myself from a potential hug. I'm a little fragile now and I fear that if I were hugged by him, I'd melt or cry or grab him and make out with him without thinking. And I need to think—it's what I do.

Charlie sits next to his cousin on the bench. I picture them both going over to the island for their family dinner. I imagine a close scene around a small table with fish his dad probably caught this morning.

So I close my door, put in a mix I made of songs that have places as their titles, and head back to Hadley Hall, which, for the moment, I still call home.

I think about what Arabella said about an SF. I thought I

had TL (true love) but it turned out he was just an LIL (lesson in love—or loss or lameness, depending on how you look at it). Like conjugating a verb I go through all the SF's I can think of while I drive.

Summer Fling. Summer Fun. Summer Friendship. Serious Fling. Slight Freakout. Somewhat Frenzied. Silly Fool. A Summer Fling doesn't sound like a bad idea, but what if one person's SF is another's TL—then you're SF'd.

Chapter 14

"Check out how much she's in love with herself right now." Chris uses his celery stalk to gesture to a proud Lindsay Parrish who is walking with her shoulders back, displaying her tan-topped breasts for all to ogle.

"She's going crazy in the dorms," Harriet Walters adds. "And I'm not one to get easily ruffled. I'm going to petition to switch houses. I can't live in Fruckner with her."

"Yeah, you're usually Miss Reserved and undeflatable," I say and look at Harriet's face. Her eyes are wide and her mouth turned down into a full frown.

"Well, call me punctured. Lindsay's decided to take it upon herself to—and excuse my air quotes here but I have to 'govern the social situations for next year.' "

"Meaning what, exactly?" Chris asks chewing his crudités. "You have to try this dip. It's made of one hundred percent fat, I think."

I dip a carrot stick in and nod. "That's revolting."

Harriet continues, "She wants to personally check each sign-out card and give her approval."

I shake my head. "That's ridiculous—she has no authority. It's not like she's a dorm parent or anything."

Chili Pomroy pipes up from her burrito, "No, that's the thing. Lindsay has already sweet-talked her way into it. She's basically convinced all of Fruckner House that if she takes on the burden of this . . ."

"That she'll pretty much control who goes where and with whom?" I ask.

Harriet nods. "Under the guise of helping out, yes."

"That sucks," Chris says. "Can you imagine? If she lived in my dorm I'd never get out to do anything—she'd neg me just so she could watch me beg."

"That's a pretty image, thanks," Chili says.

"On that note, I have to go. I'm supposed to be home having a talk with my dad." I stress the word *talk* so it's obvious I'm dreading it.

Chris leads me away from the Dinner on the Lawn, another of Hadley's pregraduation traditions. They figure half the school is outside playing Frisbee, lusting in the open air, or generally blowing off the last week of the year, so they give in a little by moving the sit-down dinners outside on pleasant evenings. It's a nice idea, and if the food weren't so heavy on the starch (um, could there be any more potato salad and pasta salad on offer?), the whole thing would be great.

"Are you nervous?" he asks.

"About what? The talk . . . no—I've pretty much dealt with it internally—or, dealt with it as much as I can. I got back from dropping Arabella and went right home to get it out of the way, but he wasn't there."

"Did you ever think it might be hard for him, too?"

I consider this for a second. "Not really. I mean, I guess I can see how he'd feel a little . . . a little loss or something—but mainly I think he's worried about announcing something happy, like he wants to marry Louisa, when everything's been so hard. So sad."

Chris nods and sends me on my way, up the hill past Whitcomb—his dorm, and back toward my house. "Hey," he shouts. "I'm thinking either Harvard or Stanford!"

"You switch every day!" I shout back. "And don't pick a college because of a boy!" I know Chris too well to underestimate the power that his new relationship status with Alistair might have on his college choice. (Note to self: If I am ever in that situation, I must remember my own advice.)

"Stanford is a respected school! It might be perfect for me," he calls.

"And it just happens to be near Alistair's home town . . . ," I say and walk away, waving to him while shaking my head.

When I walk around to the side of the house, I find not my father sitting outside, but Henry Randall. He's sitting in one of the Adirondack chairs, looking out at the empty playing fields as though they hold a view of the ocean.

When he sees me, he stands up and smiles. "Hi, Love!"

"Hey, Henry, how are you?" It dawns on me with slight apprehension that Henry might know by now that I am not in actuality a college student. I do not attend Brown University as he assumed last fall, and though I have kept up the ruse for quite a while, he's probably about to call my bluff.

"I know from Lila Lawrence that your classes are done. Did she mention that I stopped by your dorm room?" he says and yet again I am drawn into the web of deceit. Leave it to Lila to keep it going; she probably thought she was covering for me since she does really go to Brown.

"Yeah—I was just hanging out with some friends here," I say.

"Isn't it fun to go back to your high school as an alum? I've gone back to Exeter a lot."

Um, yeah, not that I know about being a high school grad, but I nod and smile. "How'd you know where to find me?"

Henry immediately blushes and stammers, "I'm not a stalker—I asked my aunt and she and Mable, you know, got to be friends . . ."

"Yeah, Margaret came to the funeral."

Henry looks at his feet and then at me. "That's kind of why I came by. I wanted to just explain why I wasn't there. It wasn't that I—I wanted to be there."

"That's okay," I say. "I didn't expect you to be or anything. It was an overwhelming day."

"I'm sure it was but I felt bad that I didn't go—just to show my support. And I mean, I know we're not like best friends or anything, but if I were in that position I know I'd want as many comforting faces around me as possible."

He stops talking there, maybe caught up, as I am, that he

just qualified himself as "comforting" to me. It was a bold statement on his part, and one I can't really dispute.

"Thanks," I say and mean it. "That's really . . . I can't believe you came all the way over here to tell me. I really appreciate it."

Henry puts his hands on both my shoulders. He's tall and broad and, at the risk of sounding redundant, has a comforting presence. He gives me a solid hug and I hug him back. "I have to run . . ."

"Big plans?"

"Yeah—I have an eight o'clock ferry reservation," he says and watches my surprised face. "What—you thought you'd have the Vineyard all to yourself this summer?"

"Maybe," I say and unlock the door to my house. "No—actually, I kind of assumed you'd be there. Among others."

"Which others would those be?" he asks, grinning with his lips closed.

"No one in particular," I say and deflect images of Charlie.

"Just remember," he says and goes down the porch steps, "some of us are better than others."

It's this last comment I'm thinking of even after I scramble after him to give him Arabella's cell number so he can check up on her and make sure she's enjoying the minimalist comforts of our new apartment. Does Henry mean that some of the guys are better than others, specifically that he is better than anyone else? Or does he mean his comment to reflect a Preppy Power statement, such as the moneyed class is better than the . . . I don't know. I feel like I'm just about to figure it out when I flip the kitchen lights on and find a note:

> Love
> Hope you had an okay trip to Wood's Hole. Wish you'd put Arabella on the bus like we discussed. Please find me on the lawn—or, if we don't connect there, meet me @ my office.
> Your name here,
> Dad.

The fact that he wrote *your name here* gives me hope that he's not worried about our talk, just wanting to get it over with.

He's sitting behind the behemoth desk behind which every Principal Headmaster has positioned themselves for the past two hundred plus years that Hadley has been around.

"Hey, Dad," I say and knock once just for show and come into the office. It's shaped oddly due to its position in a semi-tower. The far wall behind Dad's desk is curved and the rest of the walls are straight, so the whole room feels like a church window.

"You made it back, I see," he says, finishes signing something, and turns the paper over. He often stacks things or flips memos over so I won't inadvertently see what I'm not supposed to see—not so much because he doesn't trust me, he's said in the past, but because he feels it's a burden to know too much information. It occurs to me standing here that maybe that's part of his reasoning about withholding information about my mother. "Take a seat." He uses his Hadley Hall fountain pen to gesture to a chair and I sit in it, facing him as though we're having an interview or a formal meeting.

"I feel like I'm under scrutiny," I say, then add, "Or maybe that's the wrong word."

"How so?" Dad puts the pen down and looks at me, really sees me, his daughter. "Would you rather walk instead?"

"No, this is fine—I just . . . are you mad at me?"

"Am I mad at you." Dad says it not like a question but a singsongy kind of musing. "No. I'm not angry. I'm used to this . . ."

"This being my suddenly deciding to take Arabella to the ferry?"

"Not so much that—I mean, it was a considerate act, if a little much." Dad comes out from behind his desk and stands near me. He half leans on the edge of the desk, looking at me in my knees-up for protection stance in my chair. "You're growing up, obviously, and London was another step toward your independence."

"I know. We kind of went over this before, and I know you were disappointed but it's all . . ."

"I'm going to talk right now," Dad says and rubs the stubble on his face. "In light of everything that's been going on, I made an error in not addressing your London actions sooner."

"So we're talking about this now?" I must have looked surprised because Dad throws his hands up in frustration.

"What did you think we were talking about? I've been trying to figure out a way to tell you my decision for weeks, now."

I stand up so we're more face-to-face. "I thought this was about you and Louisa."

"What about us?" Dad says. "I thought you liked her."

"I do like her," I say and am amazed how much miscommunication there's been so far. "I figured you were announcing your engagement or something."

Dad smiles and sighs at the same time. "I'm not. You can rest easy."

I defend myself by quickly saying, "No—it wasn't a problem. It was more I wanted to say it's okay—not that you need my permission or blessing . . . just that it's fine."

Dad pauses and reaches for his pen so he can fiddle with it as he speaks. "Love, have you ever felt a distance between yourself and the other Hadley students?"

"What do you mean?" I ask and wonder where this is headed. I have my arms crossed in front of me as if I'm already defiant.

"It was brought to my attention recently that you have a unique perspective here, being neither a day student nor a boarder."

I relax—I guess we are just chatting. I nod. "Yeah, it's kind of odd being in the middle of it all." Then, just in case he feels bad I add, "But I'm used to it. I guess every once in a while I think it'd be nice to have that camaraderie that the girls have in the dorms."

"I'm glad to hear you say that . . ."

Cue, massive tension and sweaty palms for Love. "Why?"

"I've made a decision. I don't want you to react right away, just think about it."

"Dad, this sounds bad—"

"As of two days after Labor Day of this year, you will be an official resident of the dorms. You will spend your senior year as a boarding student."

Time seems momentarily suspended. No wedding bells for Dad and Louisa, no white dress and new woman living in our house. Just me, not living in our house. Me living with ten or twenty or thirty girls in Deals or Lawrence House or—no way—Fruckner. With Lindsay.

Dad goes on, "It seems to me that you would benefit from being in a group. You have a solitary tendency and while I'm not trying to change that, you might find yourself opening up . . ."

"I'm not a can of corn . . . ," I say and hate the analogy I picked, but I was desperate. "This is ridiculous, Dad. My life is the regular fac-brat on campus housing . . ."

"Cordelia is a faculty brat and look what happened to her . . ."

"I'm not going to end up in rehab, Dad," I say and put my hands on my hips both for its argumentative stance and for balance. "What could I possibly gain from sharing bathrooms, having to go to bed at ten o'clock, and . . ."

"Rules. A set of rules that govern you that are not flexible." Dad puts his hand on my shoulder to be nice but I flick it off, which pisses him off. "You live your life coming and going as you please, which is fine—you can do that in college and I can't stop you. And I don't want to stop you—I want you to think about what you're doing."

"I can't believe you're accusing me of not thinking—I am an overthinker! Mable just said to me that I needed to stop thinking so much—which is it? What the hell am I supposed to do?" I start crying and wipe the tears away as fast as they come because I don't want to cry. I want to get him to change his mind.

Dad makes me sit down on the leather couch so we can attempt civility. "Boarding has many benefits: There's a communal lifestyle that brings a sense of . . ."

"Dad—do NOT try to spew the tour guide talk on me. I go here already. You can't sell it to me."

Dad gets up and walks back to his desk, shuffling papers and looking weary. "My mind is made up on this, Love. Here." He hands me his signed confirmation of place, the document that starts the new student dorm assignment process. "We don't know which dorm you'll be in . . ."

"Not Fruckner," I say and then feel as though I've given in too easily. "I'd like to go on the record as saying you're making a big mistake. You want to be close to me, but here you're pushing me away. It doesn't make any sense. Unless you'd like to get rid of me and have the house all to yourself—or for you and Louisa but I already told you it's fine."

"First of all, I'm not ready to live with Louisa. We haven't discussed that yet. And in terms of being close with you, it's the most important thing in the world to me—and I'd do anything to make our relationship stronger. Which is why I'm making the very difficult decision to have you board—"

"What, absence makes the heart grow fonder?" I ask. "I

have news for you: That's not true." Look at me and Asher, look at my own parents.

"I'm hoping we both find that a little extra space—and a few more companions for you—strengthens our bond. We're so close sometimes that I think we have the ability to shut out the world, and that's not very healthy. This will be a real preparatory year . . ."

"So that when I go to college I'll be all used to sharing toilets and waiting my turn for the shower?"

"More than that, Love," Dad says. "You'll see. You'll like living on your own before college."

"I already DID live on my own—that's what got me into trouble in the first place." My face probably looks stony. I keep my mouth in a straight line, like one of those not-happy not-sad pictures, and shake my head.

"Well, I'm sorry to hear that you disagree, but that's the way it is. Now—look. September is three months away. I'm still letting you go to the Vineyard like you planned because I promised Mable."

I sigh. Maybe I won't stick around for graduation. What's the point? I'll be jailed next fall with all of these people. Why suffer more now? "Great." I say, though it hardly sounds enthusiastic. Then it dawns on me. "Were you so suffocating recently because you knew you were kicking me out?"

"I'm hardly kicking you out," Dad protests.

"That's what it feels like," I say.

"You're a very wise, psychologically aware person, Love.

I'm sure that factored into my actions—and if I was suffocating you, I apologize. I don't mean to crowd you."

"You're either all over me or too far," I say.

"That's the kind of balance I'm hoping next year will bring."

We end the conversation by locking his office door, and my silent payer is that I won't be assigned to Lindsay's dorm. Dad's footsteps and my flip-flops echo in the empty hallway. I stop in my tracks. "Dad," I say and grab his arm so he stops and turns to me. "When did you decide this?"

Dad frowns, trying to recall. "I don't know exactly."

"Well, you mentioned it was "brought to your attention" that I was in this nonboarding nonday world, which was hardly hidden. So who showed you the light?"

Dad scratches his face and rubs his spring allergy eyes. "It's funny, actually. Right around the time of the Avon Walk—"

"I knew it. You said thank you to Lindsay for the big donation, which came, just so you know, only because her mother MADE her give it, not because she's so charitable. And to get back at me—"

Dad shakes his head. "What could Lindsay have to get back at you for?"

"There's a lot you don't understand about the inner workings of my social life here, Dad. But to simplify: Chris called Mrs. Parrish and got her to make Lindsay give money. Lindsay threatened me with some revenge but I didn't think she'd stoop to going to you . . ."

We keep walking down the hall over to the flight of stairs and out onto the quad. "Well, it might have been said as revenge, but I think Lindsay's quite astute."

"She puts the ass back in astute."

"Love—enough. She made a good point and I've listened."

I let my dad keep walking and I stop by the Stripper Pole to regain my composure. "I reiterate. Do NOT assign me to Fruckner House with her."

"It's out of my control," Dad says. "You know I don't handle the dorm assignments." He smiles at me, thinking it's all okay now. "I'll see you at home?"

"Not home," I say pointedly. "Your house. As of today, I don't have a home."

"You're so dramatic!" Dad says as though he's proud of it.

But I'm not being dramatic. I'm being realistic. I don't get to live at his house, I don't yet have a dorm, and I have a sublet for the summer. I am a woman with no fixed address. Free in a good way or just cut loose?

Chapter 15

♡

I am over it. I am over the fact that my fall has great potential to suck and slime me with severe college cramps, the rules and regulations of boarding life, and the intense toll on my psyche all of that will take.

But rather than dwell on the enormity of that, I am instead focusing on the summer ahead of me. Graduation is tomorrow, my last college planning sesh is in two hours and, aside from my familial woes, the last item plaguing me is my project for Poppy Massa-Tonclair who phoned yesterday to "make sure I was taking time as part of the creative process, not because I couldn't think of what to do." Um, sure. I told her I had an idea and was working on it (had an idea=waited for the artistic muse to land in front of me).

As a result of my newfound (possibly temporary) close-to-summer sensation of happiness, I am blaring the song of the moment, "Black Coffee in Bed" by Squeeze, and singing at the top of my range when two things happen at once:

Arabella calls and squeals with laughter into the phone and Jacob knocks on the door, witnessing my vocalizing and my packing (read: aimlessly shoving various articles of clothing and linens into big duffel bags, then taking some out and shoving it in again).

"Hey," I say into the phone and motion for Jacob to come in. "Find a seat if you can," I say to him.

"Oh, do you have a boy in your bedroom?" Arabella stresses the bed part of bedroom and I quickly turn down the volume of my cell phone so Jacob can't hear what Arabella is saying. "Oh, is it Jacob?"

Good call on the volume thing. "Uh-huh," I say, trying to make it sound like I'm talking about socks or something equally banal. "That's correct."

"Is he *in your bedroom* in your bedroom or just in your bedroom?"

"You sound insane. Or just repetitive," I respond and try to switch gears (oh, driving analogy—images of me on the open road). "What's happening at the café?"

I watch Jacob settle in on the floor near my bed. He could've sat on the bed itself—arguably it's the least cluttered spot in the room (both figuratively and literally) but maybe he feels that the implications of that seatage are too much, so the platonic floor is where he rests, nestled in among my shorts, T-shirts and—oh, my sexy bra. While shopping in London, Monti—Arabella's mother—insisted she purchase me a fancy bra and underwear set. It's less fancy than it is slutty, but the price tag begs to differ. The price tag that is still on the lingerie because I never had a chance to wear it.

"The usual—Doug and Ula disagree about everything

down to what size napkins are the best, but Ula's heading back to Slave to the Grind because apparently she's got some clause in her contract that says she has to oversee that place."

"Yeah, Mable mentioned something about that. But what about you? Are you having fun yet or is it all business and no play?" I try to think of a way to hide my slut-bra from Jacob who is observant and close enough to the item to see it now. Maybe if we were closer friends or maybe if we had no past I would just let him find it and ogle it, but it's too hard to explain—that I'm not the kind of person who wears fancy bras with matching lacey revealing underwear, but I'm not opposed to it, either. That the items are just in my room, they're not really mine in the sense of emotional ownership.

Arabella laughs. "Can you hear that? Those were waves."

"You're at the beach?" I ask and check my watch. "Aren't you supposed to be working?"

"Yes, madam, but Doug told me he'd cover for me so I could explore the island."

"Did you rent a bike? I'm bringing mine and Mable's old one for you," I say. How many things do I have connected to her? How many memories attached to everyday objects?

"Actually, I got a ride!" Arabella laughs and I respond by picking up a pile of unfolded T-shirts and drop them almost on top of Jacob's head, creating a bit of a ruckus, but also covering the bra.

Jacob looks up at me from his position on the floor with a curious expression on his face. "Is this a subtle hint that you'd like me to fold your clothing?"

I shake my head and say, "No—sorry. Um, I'll be off in one minute." I wish he weren't so damn cute—no, not cute. Gorgeous. He used to be cute, and then his whole physical presence changed. He looks similar to my last-year's memories of him, but better, older, bigger, hotter than I remember from last year.

"Hey, Love!" A male voice gets on the line.

"Hello?"

"It's Henry," he says. "Hope you don't mind that I borrowed your friend."

A rustling puts Arabella back on. "Henry was kind enough to show me around."

"Giving you a private, guided tour?" I ask, trying to remain neutral but not entirely succeeding.

Arabella lowers her voice. "Are you upset?" She lowers her voice to a small whisper. "It's not like anything's happening. In fact, I think someone's got a thing for you."

Without thinking of my guest I ask, "Who has a thing for me?"

Arabella's tone shifts and she speaks in her overenunciated voice to let me know she's being listened to. "So, yes, everything is just fine. I'm heading back to the café shortly. We can talk about this more later."

"Okay," I say, then add, "I'll call you later today or tomorrow." I don't mention that I want to check up on her, because that would be annoying even if it's truthful, but the thought of being the worker bee in the café this summer while she's off getting tanned (or hmm) in the dunes doesn't exactly thrill me.

Or maybe I'm jealous—of her with Henry? I make a face at myself in the mirror and hang up the phone, wondering what the summer has in store.

"So, trouble in paradise?" Jacob asks.

"That was Arabella. She's already on the Vineyard and . . ." I look at him. "And you couldn't possibly be interested in the details, so I'll spare you."

"I am, though," Jacob says and runs his fingers through his hair. Lucky fingers. Enough—I have to think of him as my buddy. My pal. My friend. He grins. "Tell me the details of your life."

I sit next to him, aware that somewhere under me is my slut-bra. "The details. Huh. Well, I got the great news that I'll be one of your kind this fall . . ."

"A male?" Jacob narrows his eyes.

"A boarder."

"To what do we owe this honor?" He taps some rhythm on his knees and I feel tempted to ask what song he's fake-percussioning.

"That honor is courtesy of my father who feels the dorm life will do wonders for my psyche." I go over to my desk and get the mix I completed for Jacob, the one I've almost handed over a bunch of times but haven't. "Here. I owed you one, so consider this my debt paid."

Jacob studies the case. "No liner notes?"

"No. And it's not just because I forgot. It's so that you don't ruin the surprise and see the songs before you hear them."

Jacob smiles at me in his quiet way and laughs. "That's so you."

"In a bad way?" I ask and sit next to him.

"No—in a quirky, nice way."

See, how can we have exchanges like this and be just friends? Or rather, how can we have exchanges like this with me lusting after him and wanting to lean forward and kiss him and still have the label platonic hanging over us? I can't quite get there. But then, it's what he wants; there's been no overture of romance on his part. In fact, there's a rumor swirling about Jacob having spent a night in Deals last week with an unknown senior girl. Someone apparently saw him climbing down the fire escape at dawn, but then it might not have been Jacob.

"Are you excited for summer?" I ask and sound very yearbooky.

"Excited might be overstating it a little, but I'm ready to be out of here if that's what you mean."

"No, I meant more than that. At this point we're all ready to be free of the hallowed halls of Hadley—and alliteration—but I haven't heard you talk about your summer plans that much." I say this like we've been spending every minute together and he's yet to express his delight but maybe he's so cool and mellow he just doesn't get worked up about plans.

Jacob turns away and looks out my window. "The thing is I'm not completely clear on my plans at this moment."

"Care to elaborate?"

Jacob sighs. "Not really."

I wish I could take back the mix. Not because it's too this or too that but because I can't control his reaction to it, or rather I can't control what he'll think of my thinking. Maybe it will make him aware that the friend label isn't entirely accurate or maybe he'll be conceited and shrug it off or maybe he won't listen to it. But it's too late.

Jacob turns back to me, his eyes looking for a minute at my lips. "So I was wondering . . ." If I could kiss you? What the deal is with your English bloke? If you're still a virgin? " . . . if you have any spare songs lying around."

I pick up a sock and fling it in the air. "Like just sitting here doing nothing?"

"Yeah, songs you've written that don't have a tune." He waits for me to fill in the rest, with his eyebrows raised. When I don't because his question doesn't click with me, he goes on, "To pair with my stuff? Get it?" He Tarzan points to me. "You lyrics. Me music."

"Oh, that!" I sit and think, then spring to action. "They're not really finished, per se. You recall or maybe you don't, I'm not sure, that I always had a little trouble finishing the songs I started. So I have lots of lines or couplets but not many complete songs."

Jacob follows me over to the other side of my room where my bag of books and journals is ready to be packed into the Saab for the summer. I pick up my journal and flip through, hoping he can't read my messy writing from where he is.

"That's quite a book," he says.

"I know—it's really long. Mable bought it for me when I first started here and it's funny, because there's only two pages left. When I was in London, it was almost done, and now it's almost almost done. And there's just so much in here, you know. Time, me, change . . ."

"What did you just think of?" he asks and stares at me.

"Um . . ." My mouth hangs open. "I think I just solved a problem." I shut the book and suddenly need to have my room to myself so I can figure out if my solution is viable. "Jacob, can I write down some lyrics? I mean, you're not going to perform them or anything, right? But I'm happy to lend them to you . . ."

Jacob backs away from me. "Sure."

"I'm not trying to make you leave," I say.

"No, I understand I just wanted to come by and . . ."

I nod, cutting him off. "I might leave before graduation tomorrow."

Jacob's face registers what I interpret as disappointment; then he asks, "Are you coming to Crescent Beach?"

Crescent Beach. The biggest party of the year. The height of hookups and heartaches. The place we broke up after sophomore year.

"No," I say.

"No you weren't planning on it or no definitively?"

"Neither—just no," I say. I can't say more without going over everything, our past, our right now, my ambiguous feelings, wondering what his intentions are.

"Oh—well, I had thought we'd have a chance to talk more there."

Talking at Crescent Beach is akin to rolling in the sand together, like if someone asks you if you want to talk somewhere, it's the most blatant code around. So does he mean talk there or talk there? Oh my God, I'm driving myself crazy.

"In case I don't see you," I say, "have an exciting summer."

"You, too," he says and pulls back to look at me long enough that I am sure he will do it—just give in and put his hand on my head and pull me in to kiss him. But he doesn't. He looks at me and says, "Thanks for the mix. And don't forget the mainland."

"What does that mean?" I ask and can still feel his hug on me.

"Nothing—I read it once, I think. How there's some island phenomena where you can just get so sucked in to life there that you forget there's anything back on the mainland."

"I'll try to remember that," I say. "But I won't be holed up there for the entire time—I do have to tour colleges. Or at least visit a few."

"Me, too," Jacob says.

"Try not to climb out too many dorm windows," I say, risking the rumor mention just to see what he'll do.

"I'll try to take the stairs next time," he says.

"So it's true?" I ask and feel a pull in my gut at the thought of him sliding in and out of someone's window, room, or bed.

"Is it terrible if it is?" he asks, not answering.

"Terrible might be a bit strong," I say.

Then we both laugh and try to shake off sexual tension. But it's impossible. If you could see it, see the various feelings between us, if they were color-coded, we'd have blue and red and purple and yellow wavy lines emanating out and connecting us.

"Are you going to the dinner tonight?" I ask and can see the white chairs being set up on the large lawn for The Gala Under the Stars welcome dinner for parents and alums, graduates, and soon-to-be-seniors.

"No," he says.

"No you're not planning on it or no definitively," I ask pushing his words back at him.

"No definitively," he says. "I have to go to Logan."

I assume he means to pick up his mother who lives in Geneva or Genoa or someplace, so I offer, "I could drive you if you want."

Jacob says, "Thanks but I think I'll take the T. I wouldn't want you stuck there while I deal with baggage claim."

The campus bell chimes, reminding me my college meeting is soon and my possible idea for my PMT project awaits my further thoughts.

"Bye," we say to each other and don't add anything. I just turn back to my cluttered room and he turns to go down the spiral staircase and back out into the world, away from the little island of my room.

"Have you considered Brown University?" Dad asks as I walk past his study on the way to meet with my dear college counselor.

I pause in the doorframe and make allusions to my fake enrollment at that prestigious place. "I've, um, actually spent a little time there . . . with Lila Lawrence. And I'm not sure it's the right place for me."

"Oh—well, remember that Providence is only an hour away."

"Is that the recommended distance for optimal parent-child relations?" I ask and I mean it as a joke but considering the boarding school problem, it sounds sarcastic.

"I just think you might like the faculty," Dad says. "And what's in your hand there? A yearbook?"

I tuck the heavy book under my arm. It's covered by a brown padded envelope and already addressed, but I don't want to discuss it with him, so I say, "It seems like everyone wants to go to Brown—it's the creative Ivy." I picture the current junior class (of which I am only pseudoly a part) lined up—probably three-quarters are applying to Brown, even if it wasn't on their SIBOF list of suggested schools.

Dad looks at me seriously. "You know, there's no rule that says you have to decide anything right now."

"That's fine to say, Dad, but I have to actually figure it all out by fall." I tie my sweatshirt around my waist and hide my bra strap under my tank top.

"And I'm sure you will." Dad looks at my outfit. "You won't need the sweatshirt; it's supposed to reach eighty-eight degrees today."

I smile at Dad's affinity for the weather. He likes to know the predictions and patterns as though a cloud or drop will have some grand effect on his day. I drop my sweatshirt on the floor in a show of weatherly solidarity. "This report brought to you by David Bukowski . . . I'm loving the sunshine, I have to say." I shrug. "Who knows, maybe I'll wind up going to some school out west."

Dad doesn't react, doesn't say no or suggest an equally exciting eastern alternative, but I watch his hand tense around the
arm of his chair—a giveaway. So, he wants me to stay close—
but not too close. "Say hi to Mrs. Dandy-Patinko for me and
try to get back here by four so we can go through the stuff."

Dad won't say Mable's stuff. He won't refer to sifting
through her left-behind clothing and papers and furniture and
books as anything but a chore that needs to be taken care of. I
offered to do it myself but he wouldn't let me. I still don't
know if this is because he feels a parental duty to carry the burden of the emotionally loaded act of clearing out someone's
apartment after they've died or because he thinks I'll find
something there that I'm not supposed to. Maybe I'm just
reading too much into the whole thing as is my usual
tendency.

But I feel the suspicion strongly enough that I tell him,
"You know what? I have to do a couple of errands—pick up
some sunblock and hair things at the drugstore, so why don't I
just meet you there?"

"Sure," Dad says, "Sounds fine."

I leave with my protected envelope under my arm and
head to my college counseling session knowing I will cut out
just early enough so I get to Mable's apartment before Dad
does—just in case there's something there for me to find.

Yet again, my college counseling session has wound up being
a counseling session without the college focus.

"I think it makes perfect sense that you're having difficulties choosing," Mrs. Dandy-Patinko says, her gingham outfit defying her downwardly turned mouth. "You're at a point in your life that's meant to be fun and exciting, with possibilities at your feet, but you've had such a loss . . ."

I nod and my eyes well up. When strangers—or near-strangers—are kind to me I always feel exposed. "Making big decisions right now doesn't feel right."

"I agree—I think you should do this. First, we have a nice, solid list of schools here. I'll set up your visits for you and when you get back, in the fall, we can reconvene and talk. By then you'll have had a whole summer to recoup and relax . . ."

Images flip by as she speaks: me on the ferry with the wind at my back pushing my hair forward, the café, serving scalding drinks and iced blendeds while goofing around with Arabella.

"I hope I can relax this summer," I say.

"You're going to the Vineyard, correct?" Mrs. Dandy-Patinko asks. "Look up my brother. He's a potter there."

She hands me a brochure that shows a fuzzy photo of a guy behind a pottery wheel and some mugs for sale. "Thanks," I say and slide it into my pocket.

"He's a throwback to an easier time—a real seventies simpleton. But he does make beautiful mugs and bowls."

Sounds like he smokes a few, too, I want to add, but I don't. I like the idea of being a bell-bottomed pottery person living full-time on the Vineyard. Maybe I will stop by and get a mug for myself—yeah, I like that idea, too, of having my ritualistic coffee cup that I use every morning at the café.

"So it's not crazy to be looking all the way out west at

UCLA and Northwestern and then that whole cluster of schools here?"

"Why UCLA?"

"Los Angeles seems like an interesting place . . ." It's all I can come up with for the moment because if I say the real reason, the fact that Martin Eisenstein is out there with a maybe-voice thing for me, I'll sound ridiculous.

"I would have thought you'd be more the San Francisco type," Mrs. Dandy-Patinko says.

"Well, add that to the list then—I could fly from LA to San Fran I guess, depending on the cost . . ." I look at my list again. "Maybe I should reconsider Williams. My friend Chris said it's like a bigger version of Hadley Hall."

Mrs. Dandy-Patinko clicks her tongue and shakes her head. "What's so interesting is that one person's prep school hell is another person's ideal college. You just can't tell. You can be best friends with someone and visit the same school and have very different reactions."

I nod. "I know. I guess . . . if you don't mind planning all the visits for these dates . . ." I hand her a printout of my summer calendar. It's basically empty except where I've penciled in "college visits" in August.

"I'll try," she says and pats my hand. "But those last couple of weeks are the toughest to get appointments. Everyone's touring then. So you might have to squeeze in an interview or two before then."

I check my watch, feeling the need to beat my dad to the sorting through process. "Thanks, I really appreciate your help."

"I know you do," she says and stands up to show me out.

"Not just the school stuff—the other issues, too," I say and she watches me go.

I walk to my car thinking good-bye Maus Hall, good-bye quad, good-bye Stripper Pole, not because I'm leaving this instant, but because as of tomorrow morning I am out of here. I decide I have just enough time to zip to the tiny post office at the end of campus that serves both the school and the town of Fairfield. Of course, when I get there, I'm annoyed to find:

"We don't ship internationally."

"But—I have to get this out—overnight." I hold up my parcel as proof that my academic life hangs in the balance. "It's due tomorrow but I have a couple days of grace period because I'm here and LADAM is . . ."

The postal lady nods in sympathy but then reverses her head's direction and shakes. "Can't do anything about it. Rules are rules."

Fuck rules, I want to scream but figure this won't help my chance of posting my package. I turn around, gripping my parcel tightly in both hands, and wonder if I have time to go to the post office that's not too far from Mable's place.

"In a hurry?" This from Jacob, who looks at me as though he's planned on seeing me. He never seems surprised to find me near him. I on the other hand always feel shocked that he's real—or that we bump into each other or that he shows up at my room. I'm not sure why this is, but it's a feeling I've definitely become more aware of recently.

"Yeah, I'm late—well, not yet and I just found out that you can't mail things internationally from here," I say.

"Only letters—not packages," Jacob says, informed. Suddenly it occurs to me that he could be well aware of the postal rules here. . . . Maybe he sent or still sends international correspondence with a bevy of foreign babes. I banish the thought.

"I'm actually about to take off," I say and step past him so I can hurry hurry hurry.

"For good?" he pulls back like I slapped him.

"Just for the summer . . . graduation's not . . . anyway, I guess I'll see you in the fall." Then I remember his Logan excursion. "Did you get to the airport and back okay?" I ask and hope he offers to introduce his mother. Why do I hope this? One of those "if he introduces me to his mom then he must like me or consider me a good friend or something" games.

Jacob blushes. "Logan was fine. Yeah." He opens the door to the post office and bites his top lip. "Any chance you've reconsidered Crescent Beach?"

I hold the package with one hand and lift my hair off my neck with the other. Then I pretend to shake a Magic Eight Ball and read the response, "Highly Doubtful."

"Got it," Jacob says. "I won't ask again."

He comes over, gives me a quick kiss on both cheeks—how very Euro—and we part ways. "Hey," I say, "it's like that song . . ."

He looks at me over his shoulder, his green eyes catching my gaze and holding it. "Yeah—I know the one." He whistles *though we've got to say good-bye for the summer* . . . I wish I could remember the rest of the lyrics.

Then, when I'm back in the car, I do. The song is about saying good-bye for the summer, promising to meet up again in the fall. I sing out loud and am glad Jacob isn't around to hear me.

Good-bye, campus, see ya, semicircle of buildings and dorms I won't have to deal with for three solid months, ciao cheesy yearbook images of blond girls on the wall by the quad, jocks in full action mode on the field, the drama crowd in stage makeup, and the candid shots that highlight cliques and display now broken-up couples. I sound jaded, but I'm not. Even though I make fun of the yearbook, it means something—it has a full year cycle in it—the you you were in September all the way to the you that's holding the completed book now. My yearbook remains unsigned but stashed in my trunk so I can show it to Arabella.

Every step I take is one step closer to the Vineyard and Arabella. Arabella who was supposed to call me but hasn't. Or was I supposed to call her? No, it's her turn. Who cares. I call her cell phone but don't leave a message when she doesn't pick up.

Then I try the café. When Doug answers he says "Slave to the Grind Two" so fast it sounds like "Slimed to the Greentoop," which I make a mental note could be a song title. Songs—songs I need to "lend" to Jacob. Wait—back to the phone.

"Hi, Doug, it's Love Bukowski."

"Ah, the famous Love," he says, unaware perhaps that he has said "the famous Love" each time he's spoken to me and it's past getting old. "We'll be seeing you tomorrow, I hear."

"Yes, I think so. Is Arabella around?"

With the sound of the milk frother in the background, Doug says, "Nope. She's left for the day."

"Oh—I'll try her upstairs then. Do you know that number?" There's a phone number for the apartment but we are so reliant on cells I haven't bothered to write it down.

"She's not there, either. She's staying at your friend's house."

"My friend?"

"Henry," Doug says as though he's reading it from a piece of paper, which maybe he is, "Henry Randall's. She said it was more comfortable there."

Henry Randall's eleven-bedroom mansion is more comfortable than our linenless, pillowless, unair-conditioned tiny apartment? Really? No shit. Thanks for telling me. I say this in the polite way, my overly cheery "Thanks, Doug!" like he's provided me with anything but annoying info and hang up.

I drive to Mable's, gripping the wheel like it's Arabella's shoulders. Is she just having fun or hooking up with him? And if it's the latter, does it bug me?

Do I expect to have anything romantic with Henry? My solid answer is maybe. I can't rule it out. But more than that, I was hoping Arabella would like our simple flat, enjoy using the same one pot for pasta and oatmeal. But maybe she's too highbrow. Or maybe I'm just not there yet, not yet in full "serve the coffees all day, hot tub and bonfire at night" mood.

•   •   •

I get to the post office and fill out the customs form, hesitating where it says contents. Do I write schoolwork? Academic papers? Final project? Or just printed matter?

   I go with the last one and slip my letter in before I seal it up.

To: Poppy Massa-Tonclair

From: Love Bukowski

Enclosed please find my novella. I know, it's not exactly what one might call traditional, but please allow me to explain. It's not really a true novella, nor is it poetry, nor song. But this, my journal, isn't a cop-out. On the contrary, this journal is the truest part of me, the most real story of my life so far. I've edited nothing, except for a couple of names for privacy's sake (theirs, not mine), and if you just give it a chance, you'll find everything you asked me to write about is all there. That I'm all in there. Please consider it my final paper, my big project. You asked for the truth, and this is it. I'm sending it registered mail; it's hard to part with it—but it's yours for the reading.
Thanks, Love.

Once I pay for the postage and hand it over, it's as though a huge weight has been lifted from my mind and shoulders. My past, my project, is out in the world. And I am temporarily rid of it. I never did give those lyrics to Jacob and now I'm glad I didn't. He can hook up with random boarders or date darling sophomore debutantes, but he can't have all those parts of me. My words are mine—or now, Poppy Massa-Tonclair's. And I can move forward rather than rereading and trying to make sense of what happened prior to now.

Using my emergency key I have yet to free from my key ring, I unlock the front door to Mable's apartment and go upstairs. Through the window below, Ula is visible in her matronly apron (hey, is it a wonder that those two words rhyme?) and Slave to the Grind is bustling with the presummer need for creamy iced coffee and frozen lemonade. I want to peer in and see if the tin we set up for a big donation to the Avon Foundation has been filled, but I don't let myself get off track. Instead, I take the steps two at a time, unlock the other door, and push it open with my knee.

It's not the first time I've been back. Mable asked me to come back and get her a book or a sweater at different points, but it's the first time I've been here alone since the funeral. And though I expected to walk in and find some box—not necessarily with a bow around it—with my name on it, there's nothing. No dishes in the sink, no box of information for me. Just Mable's old things. The detritus left behind after a life is finished. I walk around, lightly touching things, leaving my fingerprints on the dusty television top, moving one of her throw pillows back to the couch from where it had fallen on the floor.

Only now do I see how empty her place is. Nothing's been

removed but before, when I used to visit, when we ate lo mein tucked up together on the couch or listened to her old albums on the floor in her room, the apartment felt full, crammed with stuff. But it wasn't—that was just Mable and her lively presence, I guess. I wander through, expecting to hear my dad's footsteps any second. Then I remember something—something weird.

I look under the sink where all the cleaning supplies are. In back of the half-empty bottles of blue Windex and Mop & Glo ("You be mop, I'll be glo," Mable used to say and we'd laugh our asses off as we cleaned and took on other personalities) is a ceramic pot (hey, maybe it was made by Mrs. Dandy-Pantinko's brother! Or maybe my life just isn't quite that circular).

I lift the lid and find a twenty dollar bill—Mable always said to have an emergency twenty at hand—and a key. I take out the key and hold it in my palm. It's one of those tiny ones, from a filing cabinet, and I remember last fall finding Mable shoving something in a drawer and telling me to mind my own business, which isn't something she did all that often.

I go to her desk in her bedroom and think how sad the unmade bed looks. I start to pull the sheets up but then feel freaked out and sad at the same time—won't it look worse if it's made? And when was the last time someone slept here, anyway? The key unlocks not the first, not the second, but the third cabinet drawer I try and inside is . . . just a stack of old electricity bills.

What was I hoping to find? A message from her or pictures, something I don't have? I don't know what. But possibly this is one of the feelings you're left with, just this aching need for more than you can't ever satisfy.

I close the drawer and start looking through the book-shelves for the few items I will keep. Mable left instructions that all her household goods be donated to charity after I had a chance to look through and take anything I wanted. So all the albums will come home with me even though I don't have a record player, some books, maybe an article of clothing if I can handle having it. The material objects aren't what I need and I guess Mable knew that, and it's not like keeping her yellow chipped teapot will help me. But maybe it will, so I grab it and put it in my pile of stuff to keep—I can take it to the Vineyard and think of her while I sip cranberry tea out of a mug made by a hippy potter.

"Hey, Dad," I say without turning around. I heard his key in the door and the big footsteps on the stairs.

"Not quite."

I turn around and see Miles, with his still defeated face, plaid cotton shirt with the sleeves rolled up, and pants too heavy for such a warm day. "Hi, Miles, what're you doing here?"

"Your dad called me to help lift—I'm just a mover, I guess."

"You know you were more than that," I say but then don't say anything else. It's not my place to dissect their on-again, off-again romance nor its remains.

He looks around and notices the cabinet under the sink is

open. He closes it with his foot and looks at me. "Wrong place."

Miles has never been a man of many words. In fact Mable used to say he spoke in two word sentences and I think she was right. "Meaning?" I say, giving him one word for his two.

"Record player." Two words.

"Oh." One word. I walk to the record player and when I see what's underneath the dark plastic cover, I talk in a steady stream of many more words than one.

"Oh my God, this is just the kind of thing I was really hoping to find, like maybe what you'd have in a movie except this is obviously my real life. But I was—am—just so happy. And sad. But tell me what it is . . ."

I hold a big, sealed envelope that has my name on the front. The contents of this packet are unknown to me and I start to undo the tab at the back flap when Miles stops me. "She made me promise."

"Promise what?"

"When I went to see her all those times, at Mass General . . . it wasn't just to visit. She had some things she wanted you to know, some items that . . . but it was under the condition that you not just tear into it."

I stop myself from ripping the thing open and rub my palms together so I won't be tempted. "So how long do I have to wait?" I tear up a little and my voice wavers. "I don't know how long I can—I mean, years?"

Miles responds. "No. She had a plan. Let your summer unfold. That's what I'm supposed to tell you. *Unfold*. And then this part . . ." He points to the envelope. "You can open when you start your college tour."

"She was supposed to go with me," I say sadly, imaging her singing in the passenger seat.

"Now she will be," he says. "Really."

Dad comes in right when Miles is saying really and stares at the big envelope. I'm in defensive mode, so I clutch it to my chest and say, "It's for me. Mable left it *for me*."

"I know she did," Dad says and even Miles looks surprised. "I knew her too well to think she'd give up having the last word about anything . . . Are you opening it?"

"Not now," I say. "I'm supposed to let my summer *unfold*."

Downstairs at Slave to the Grind, Louisa sips her latte, waiting.

"Dad's still dealing with the papers up there," I say and sit down next to her at the counter that faces the street.

"He's having a rough time," she says and looks to see if I'll agree or not.

I nod. "We both are, but I think you're right. Maybe it's worse for him."

Louisa pushes her hair back from her faces and fiddles with the wooden stirrer. "I don't think you can really compare one person's grief to another's . . . but it's my feeling that David— your dad—feels very alone."

I consider what she said and then respond, "You mean because he's been a single parent and now his only version of a co-parent is gone?"

"Partially that. But also—you. You're leaving, and that's rough on him."

"But I'm supposed to leave," I say. "Kids grow up and change and move on, right?" As I say it, I feel sad, guilty, and wonder if being apart this summer is a good thing.

"Of course you're supposed to move on. That's the mark of good parenting, that you'll be self-sufficient and confident without him. But it doesn't make it easier from his point of view—he'll miss you."

"I'll miss him, too," I say. "Thanks."

Louisa points to the street where my dad waves to us to come outside. "For what?"

I hop down from the stool and wait for Louisa to wrap one of her trademark scarves around her neck and throw out her coffee cup. "For being there—for him. And for me, too, I guess." I don't want the moment to be too public service announcement, too cloying, so I shrug.

Louisa shrugs back, aware that if we push too hard at closeness, our carefully built relationship might topple. "No problem. Now, if you don't mind giving me a ride back to Cambridge, that'd be great."

"Sure," I say and we head outside to where my dad is, in our newly formed, but somewhat workable triangle.

Back at home, Dad and I sit with the video on PAUSE.

"Are you sure you don't want to?" I ask. I wanted him to see the final cut of my video project of Mable.

Dad shakes his head. "I'm sorry, kiddo. I'm just not ready."

"You don't have to be sorry—I get it. But it's not supposed to be a eulogy. It's supposed to celebrate her life." Dad nods but looks so sad. "Although I guess it would have been better to film before she got sick."

"I think you did a wonderful thing, Love. And I really do want to see it. At some point. Maybe in the fall, okay?" He doesn't add that this summer is supposed to heal us or make it better or just put time and days in between the loss and the present, but I know what he's saying.

"And I know Mable told you more about . . ." He very obviously has trouble deciding what to say next. "Gal-adriel." My turn to nod at him. "And I guess I think it's time you did know more. But . . . ," he sighs. "But it's a lit-tle scary for me."

I furrow my brow. "Why? It's not as though she has any-thing over you, Dad."

"Maybe not," he says, "but can I ask one thing?"

"Of course," I say and hope he doesn't ask me not to look for answers, ask questions, or find out who Galadriel is.

"Just remember who stayed," Dad says and remains next to me on the couch until I squeeze his hand and we go get some dinner.

Arabella's email contains exactly one word and one picture. Standing in knee-deep reed-filled water, fishing pole in hands, is Charlie, sans shirt and with a look of intense focus that makes me long to be the subject of such a gaze. Arabella has clearly taken the picture without Charlie noticing—and you can only see part of his face; all of his body, and his feet are, of course, water-covered. For a second, I am in that water with him, slicking myself to his bare chest; then I remember I'm looking at a picture whose caption reads "SF."

Summer Fling? More? Neither. Remembering that he bailed on me before and would be thus likely to again, I switch my computer off and go to bed. Alone.

"It wouldn't be for long, probably two weeks at most. Maybe sixteen days," Dad says the next morning and moves the stack of travel books to the side so we can actually see each other at the table.

"It's fine. I said it's fine. There's no reason to rush back from Belgium or . . . Where else are you going?"

"I'd like to hike the Hebrides in Scotland—very rugged, very beautiful."

Louisa finishes her cereal and says, "Which is fine with me as long as we balance it out with a little time in a city."

"I hear Edinburgh has a festival," I say, thinking of Asher and his artistic troupe.

Dad immediately says, "No—not Edinburgh—somewhere new." Not that I knew he'd been there. But then, considering my big package from Mable there's a lot I have yet to find out.

"Maybe Capri," Louisa says and reaches for the guide.

I hug my dad good-bye and give a quick not-really-a-hug to Louisa. Dad helps me out to the car with the last of my bags and eyes my precious package from Mable.

"I can't stop you from reading all that," he says.

"Would you want to?" I ask and watch his face.

"Not really. Just know that I wanted to protect you—I still want to protect you. . . ."

I listen to this last part and wonder if he'll protect me from the dorm hell that awaits me in the fall. But I know he means protect me from getting hurt, being left. "You can't protect me from everything," I say to him gently and hug him tightly. I expect he'll be annoyed at this, or bring up the fact that I've told him twice now that I feel constrained here—by him, by loss, by memories—and by school.

BUT. But. But he doesn't. He helps me lift my big pack onto my back and steadies me when it seems I might fall down. "Hey, you did with my physical balance what you do to my emotional being," I say in a Zen master voice.

"I'm proud that you trust me with your feelings," Dad says. "Even if I don't always agree with them."

"I don't want to board next year," I say, parroting myself yet again. Like a toddler who wants another cookie I somehow feel that if I ask enough times he will change his mind.

"You have no choice in this matter," he says. And then, I suspect so we don't end on this note he says, "I'll miss you."

"Me, too," I say. "A lot can happen in three months."

"Not quite three," Dad says and sits on the porch watching me get in the car. I put the pack on the passenger seat, my pretend boyfriend. I will name him Jim. Jim my pretend backpack boyfriend. It's pathetic enough that I grin. "I'll be there in August for Illumination Night."

I haven't seen it since I was little, but all the gingerbread cottages in Oak Bluffs are lighted up by thousands of Japanese lanterns of all colors. The pictures make it seem unreal, like something from a fairy tale.

"Right," I say.

"And you can always come back if you need to," he says and then, as though the thought is too terrible, he covers with, "But you won't have to. It'll be great."

I drive a few feet and then pull the hand brake. "Dad— Mable said to ask you something."

"What was that?" Dad asks from the porch.

"My name. She said you'd tell me about my name."

Dad stands up, stretches his long arms up toward the sky, and walks barefoot over to my opened window. "The Beatles."

"When you were in London?"

Dad nods. "She knew someone at Apple Records . . ."

"So I could have been named Macintosh or something?"

"We were happy—and it made sense."

"So which song is it then?" I ask, feeling my moniker mystery untangling.

"All You Need Is Love," he says. I take it from his expression that he knows now this isn't totally true. But it's a wonderful thought.

"Thanks," I say and put my hand on his, then release the brake and go.

Neither of us cries—about the good-bye nor about Mable—we just look at each other from his place on the porch and mine behind the wheel. I steer out the driveway. With my fully crammed car, I can't see what I've left behind in the rearview mirror.

• • •

A brief stop on central campus for:

"Oh, I hate saying good-bye," Chris says. "I can't believe you're bagging graduation."

"Well, you do look dapper," I say, "but I'm going to pass. There's only so much pomp and circumstance I can handle."

Chris is dressed in the grad day duds of white trousers and a blue blazer and the Hadley crested tie. Juniors who are about to be seniors wear a purple iris on their lapels (boys) or carry a long-stemmed iris (girls). Chili is wearing a regular sundress because she can't march in the processional since she's not yet a full student.

"Just think—this time next year you'll be done with soph-omore year," I say. Then I clunk my forehead and say to Chris, "and we'll be graduating. Shit."

"Hey, Love! Glad to hear you'll be one of us next term," Lindsay Parrish shouts from across the street, her bright white trouser suit elegant and crisp against the backdrop of trimmed lawn.

"Don't bet on it," I yell back with a smile so she thinks I'm just thrilled. Lindsay walks off with her uptight mother at her side, and just for good measure turns around and says, "And if I don't see you before the summer, remember this!" She gives me an exaggerated finger behind her back and Chris just joins me as I smile and wave, parade-style.

"Nice—well handled."

"Just because there's no way for me to get out of boarding,

it doesn't mean she deserves a summer of satisfaction . . . ," I say.

Chris gives me a puerile grin. "No—you're the one who deserves that." Then he thinks. "Same goes for me . . . I just have to get to the Fourth of July. . . . ."

"And your romantic week with Alistair," I say completing his thought. "I hope it's everything you want it to be."

"Same for you," Chris says and gives me a kiss on the cheek.

Chili hands me a piece of paper. "I know I gave you this before, but just so you have it—call me. I get down to the Vineyard next week. Haverford's coming, too." She throws in that last part without knowing it will make Chris respond.

"Really? I thought he was working at a bank or something," he says.

Chili laughs. "Bank Street Grill," she says. "My mom is the silent partner in this really good dinner place. You should visit."

I reach my arm out the window and poke Chris. "You know you want to . . . ," I say but don't mention anything about his former or perhaps still-present feelings for Haverford.

Chili turns to me. "And *you* definitely should—I think Haverford would like that." She raises her eyebrows and I am horrified to think what that means. That Haverford is not only *not* gay but interested in little me? No—I find that very hard to believe, though in other circumstances he'd be the one to make me turn my head for a recheck.

"Maybe we can all go together," I suggest and then accidentally but not lean on the horn and signal my own transport is leaving. "See you soon!"

I leave all of campus behind—it's graduation chairs and potted plants, its immaculate lawns and trays of postceremony finger foods, and somewhere, in the crowd, a wickedly grinning Lindsay Parrish who knows she won this round, and one Jacob Coleman who will head to Crescent Beach and maybe look for me—or not—but I won't be there. I will save myself from humiliation or heartache by avoiding the party altogether.

Later, I'm at the Flower Market.

Empty of carts and flower merchants stocking up for the weekend, the smells hit me with memories of being here with Mable. As a little girl I would hold her hand and kick through the fallen petals as though they were leaves from the trees. The ground is strewn with petal snow—bright pink near circles cast off from roses, longer tapers from the Gerber daisies that come in every color, and stray buds from the baby's breath.

I take a plastic bag from my pocket and use my palm to sweep the petals into it. I fill the whole thing and then bring it back to the car and drive to Slave to the Grind.

"I can't really talk right now," I say into my cell to Arabella. "I'm about to . . ."

"Neither can I," Arabella snorts and laughs. "I'm too busy doing shots of something repulsive."

"Are you going to wind up at the Vineyard ER after a night of binge-drinking? Haven't we moved beyond that phase of socializing?" I ask and adjust my rearview mirror.

"No—Henry and his money-dripping mates have brought a tiki party to the beach. I just moved out of earshot, though, so don't worry—our conversation won't be broadcast to the drunken masses."

"Well, I assume you don't call them money-dripping to their faces," I say and then fill her in on my plan. "I'm about to do it. So don't talk, just listen, and tell me afterward if you can hear the wind."

Slave to the Grind has always been on one of the windiest corners in all of Boston. Unprotected from the taller buildings—there's a law that you can't build anything over two stories in the historic district—the corner is a tunnel of gusts. The sunshine is that kind where the rays are distinct and the beams warm the windy spot where I stand. I untie the knot I made in the plastic bag and in one big shake, I dump all of the flower petals out. They take flight, swirling up and around the street, over the café and up into the sky. I cry and then smile at the same time, thinking of the beauty of the moment, the place, and Mable.

"It's amazing," I say to Arabella when the petals are still going.

She's quiet for a minute, respectful, and then jumps in.

"You know what we need?" Arabella says. "And I'm at South Beach by the way, just so you can picture me . . ."

"What do we need?" I ask and wonder if she's got her toes in the ocean, digging them into the cold wet sand, or if she's standing on one of the peaked dunes, the sea grass at her ankles.

"Mum's always saying if things don't seem pulled together, you need a theme."

"I think your mother was talking about a living room or a bed set, Bels," I say and jingle my keys against my pale thigh as I walk to the stuffed car. In another month, my legs will be shades darker, my hair shades lighter, and my spirit? Who knows. "I don't know if Mable meant a theme when she left word that I should let my summer *unfold*."

"No—even holidays or outfits or friendships can have a theme."

"So, what will the theme of the next few months be?" I ask and unlock the door.

"I've been wearing early sixties surfer gear," she says.

"And spitting out non sequiturs?" I ask and laugh. "But I'm glad to know you have Hawaiian print sarongs lying around . . ."

"And we can decorate the apartment with old surfboards and—um—leis . . . ," she says and giggles.

"I think you mean lays . . . ," I say and put the keys into the ignition but sit there, idling as we talk.

"So the theme is like Beach Boys meets silly sixties beach bunny film meets current cool," Arabella says.

"Like that Beach Boys album Mable had," I say and picture it as clearly as if it were in my hands and she were at my side. "*Endless Summer* it was called."

"Perfect," Arabella says. "Perfect. Now—I'll see you soon, K?"

"K," I respond.

I'm supposed to drive toward the Cape now, toward the island, but as I pull away from Mable's for the last time, the swirls of flower petals still arcing somewhere above me, I pause at the on-ramp to the highway. Then, without overthinking, without analyzing, I decide to delay my departure just for one night. One night meaning tonight—when I will show up at the Crescent Beach party and see what happens. I reach into the glove compartment to get a stick of rainbow Fruit Stripe gum—Mable's favorite and mine, too, despite the fact that the flavor lasts for all of ten seconds. Along with the chewing treat I pull out the pottery pamphlet from Mrs. Dandy-Patinko. As I gear up for my drive to Crescent Beach I look at the back of the brochure, really reading it for the first time, and find extra text pasted next to a picture of a wide, blue mug.

> *Love—Glad to know you are letting your summer unfold . . . or least, you're starting to look closely at things and know that even though I am not with you right now, I will never leave you.—Aunt M.*

I tuck the pottery booklet back, still folded up neatly, and put the whole pamphlet into my big, new, empty journal. I wonder for a second what the pages will hold by the Fourth of July, by Illumination Night, by Labor Day, by tomorrow morning after my adventure tonight.

With Boston behind me, I turn the car toward tonight's big bash and think of our theme: Endless Summer. It sounds poetic, pure, potential-filled. Those days of beaches and boys that

About the author

Emily Franklin is the author of *The Principles of Love* series, and two novels: *The Girls' Almanac* and *Liner Notes*.

Spring is over, school's out, but before the fall
of senior year at Hadley Hall starts,
read all about the...

Summer of Love

Coming in March 2007!

Want to know more about LOVE?

Visit www.emilyfranklin.com **for details.**